THE RIVERDALE CHRONICLES

By Charles F. Rechlin

BeachHouse
Books
www.beachhousebooks.com

BeachHouse Books
Chesterfield Missouri

Graphics Credits:

The cover design is by Dr. Bud Banis based on a stock photograph from
the Imagine! Collection by Macmillan and Company. The photograph
of the author is by Yvonne Bynum.

ISBN 1-888725-84-2 BeachHouse Books Edition
ISBN 1-888725-85-0 MacroPrintBooks Edition (large print)
Publication date February, 2003
First Printing, February, 2003

Library of Congress Cataloging-in-Publication Data
Rechlin, Charles F.
  The Riverdale chronicles / by Charles F. Rechlin.
    p. cm.
  ISBN 1-888725-84-2 (BeachHouseBooks regular-size print : alk. paper)
-- ISBN 1-888725-85-0 (MacroPrintBooks large print (16pt) : alk. paper)
  1. Golf stories, American. 2. Humorous stories, American. I. Title.

PS3618.E423R59 2003
813'.6--dc21

                      2003004231

www.beachhousebooks.com

an Imprint of
Science & Humanities Press

PO Box 7151
Chesterfield, MO 63006-7151
(636) 394-4950
sciencehumanitiespress.com

"'What are golf?' he asked, looking at me innocently.

"'Golf,' I answered. 'Oh, golf is a sort of game indulged in by the so-called upper classes and practically the entire population of Scotland and the Union League Club.'"

Thorne Smith, Out o' Luck

Acknowledgements

Grateful acknowledgement is made to the following magazines and organizations who published the original versions of the pieces indicated:
SHORT STORIES BIMONTHLY: "Partners"
WILD CHILD PUBLISHING.COM: "Neanderthal," "Golf on Trial" and "Second Chances"
CZ ONLINE: "Planet Golf"
WORDS OF WISDOM: "The Barrier," "Going for the Gold" and "Coupled"
THE PINK CHAMELEON: "The Slump"
BOONEDOGGLE PRODUCTIONS: "A Gentleman's Game"
PKA'S ADVOCATE: "The Lucky Shoes" and "The Kid"
THE ICONOCLAST: "Ace"
VERMONT INK: "A Gentleman's Game"
LINES IN THE SAND: "Second Chances"
EMOTIONS LITERARY MAGAZINE: "The Looper"

Table of Contents

PROLOGUE

AFICIONADO

A tall, gaunt figure emerges from an electric golf cart into the hot, sticky summer air. Tucking in his shirt and hitching up his trousers, he surveys the lush, green surroundings. Their breathtaking beauty is lost on him.

Shading his eyes against the glare of the mid-day sun, he peers out across the fairway, hoping against hope for a lucky bounce. Seeing nothing but pristine, finely-mown grass, he sets out to find his ball, scouring rough, scrutinizing sand traps, rummaging through bushes and under trees. Hopes fading, he wanders about aimlessly, eyes glued to the ground, like an explorer in search of a long-lost wilderness trail. He stops, shakes his head and groans. It's no use, he tells himself. It's not here.

Suddenly, he sees something gleaming on the fairway ahead. Heart racing, throat dry, he sprints toward it. Arriving at the glittering vision, he finds not his ball, but a discarded wad of chewing gum, encased in a crumpled cellophane wrapper. He falls to his knees and pounds his fists on the ground in frustration.

"Face it, Jack," his playing partner shouts from across the fairway, "you went into the ditch."

Trudging back to the cart, he grabs a wood and an iron from his bag, then begins the long trek into the dark, tree-lined ravine. Bracing himself against the muddy bank with his clubs, he slowly descends the slippery incline, like a novice skier negotiating an Alpine slope. Distracted by a bird passing overhead, he stumbles and loses his balance. Teetering helplessly, struggling to stay upright, he feels a sharp, searing pain in his thigh. His legs give way. "Whoa!" he cries as, surrendering to gravity, he topples over and slides down the hill, his clubs following him to the bottom.

I gotta be crazy, he tells himself as he gets to his feet, retrieves his clubs and brushes sticky bits of mud, grass, twigs and leaves off his brand new shirt and slacks. Four grand a year for dues, twelve hundred for carts, another thousand or two for food, clubs, balls and God-knows-what else. And the aggravation – the Goddamn aggravation!

Just then, he spots what appears to be a ball lurking in the shadows of a moss-covered rock. He hobbles toward it, steeling himself for another let-down. Bending over stiffly, he discovers that it is indeed a ball, and that, on its dimpled surface, are his initials, scrawled in *red ink. Looking up, he sees a narrow opening between the trees to the fairway beyond. A miracle! he exults. I can still make par! Momentarily forgetting his pain, he dances an awkward little jig.*

His celebration is short-lived as he realizes that the ball is nestled between two jagged stones. Why me? he implores the golf gods.

A tantalizing thought crosses his mind. Why not kick these stones away and tee up the ball on a nice tuft of grass? What would be the harm? Who would ever know?

He dismisses the idea. It wouldn't be right! It wouldn't be golf!

He grips his iron firmly. "Fore on the fairway!" he shouts as he takes his stance and prepares to swing.

He backs away. Why would any sane person try to hit from down here? Why not just go back to the tee, take a penalty stroke and hit over? Or pick up, concede the hole and move on? He mulls these alternatives. He rejects them – as usual, not quite knowing why.

"Fore up on top!" he calls out again. He addresses the ball, grounds his club and, grunting audibly, unleashes a mighty swing.

As he follows through, a clump of wet grass and mud pelts him in the face. Choking, he looks up, catching a fleeting glimpse of his ball flying through the gap in the trees. He loses it in the sun.

He scampers up the slope, scratching and clawing his way to the top. As he struggles to reach the fairway, a branch slaps him on the cheek; a pebble strikes him in the eye; the soggy ground gives way under his feet. He slips, falls, then gets back up, all the while grinding his teeth against the throbbing pain in his leg.

"Hey, nice shot, buddy!" his partner crows, grabbing him by the hand and lifting him out of the mucky abyss.

Winded, sweaty, shirt torn, slacks filthy and hair in disarray, he gazes anxiously down the fairway. There, just short of the green, lies his ball.

"It was nothing," he says modestly, trying to catch his breath. "A piece of cake."

The two return to the cart. "Say, Jack, you look a little worn out. Wanna take a break? Maybe let the group behind us play through?"

He grabs a towel and wipes his face. He grins.

"Me – worn out?" he scoffs. "Hell no! Golf's a mental game. All you gotta do is use your head. Now, let's get on with it!"

He's already thinking about his next shot.

THE PLAYERS

PARTNERS

"Golf camaraderie, like that of astronauts and Antarctic explorers, is based on a common experience of transcendence; fat or thin, scratch or duffer, we have been somewhere together where non-golfers never go."

John Updike, *Golf Dreams*

All winter long, Mother Nature held River Grove in a stranglehold. Sub-zero temperatures, blustery Northeast winds, record snowfall and gray, overcast skies battered the upscale suburban community relentlessly from December through February. And no one suffered more than the members of the Riverdale Golf and Country Club, whose lush links lay buried beneath a thick blanket of snow and ice. Patience wore thin, and tempers flared, among the Club's winter-weary membership as what seemed to be a permanent Ice Age descended upon the city.

It was, therefore, with a collective sigh of relief that, on the first day of spring, members—so long deprived of the fellowship of fairway and green—greeted a letter from the Club's General Manager announcing April 7 as "Opening Day," and inviting all men to participate in the Annual Partners Best Ball Classic. Bags were taken from storage, clubs cleaned and polished, shoes cleated and shined. Everyone looked forward to the season's kickoff event--everyone, that is, except Arthur Edwards and Wally Greer, the reigning champions.

"What are we going to do with those two?" groaned Alison Edwards as she sat having coffee with her roommate, Penny Greer, in the campus bookstore. "Dad's talking about giving up golf for stamp collecting."

"That's nothing," replied Penny. "My Dad's got the idea he should hang up his windbreaker and sun visor, and take up great books and classical music! Can you imagine?"

The two students were discussing a falling out between their fathers over Arthur's prized Toro snowblower. Wally had borrowed the device after a February storm had dumped more than a foot of snow on River Grove. Unfortunately, when he turned the ignition key and stepped on the gas, the aging contraption burst into flames. Although no one was injured, the snowblower was a total loss. Arthur, blaming Wally, demanded he buy a new one; Wally, indignant, refused. As the dispute lingered, each vowed never to speak to the other again.

The petite, sandy-haired Alison shuddered at the thought of the two men, who had spent almost every weekend for the past twenty summers playing golf together, sitting at home, "improving" themselves.

"It doesn't make sense," she said. "They'll be miserable, and, because they'll be miserable, we'll be miserable! We've got to get them back together."

Penny, a tall, thin brunette with dark brown eyes, pursed her lips pensively. "That's a tall order. They're so different. Your father's cultured and sophisticated. Mine's . . . oh, you know how he is."

Alison nodded. "It's a wonder they managed to stay partners this long . . . ."

Penny's eyes suddenly lit up, a mischievous smile crossing her face. "I've got an idea," the psyche major said. "Why don't we hold an intervention? You know, like they do in twelve-step programs. We've been studying all about them in Deviant Behavior 203. You get a bunch of people together and confront a person with his problem and the effect it's having on those around him. It works with alcoholics and addicts. Why not golfers?"

"It's an interesting idea," Alison conceded, "but . . . ."

"It's at least worth a try! What do we have to lose?"

"Nothing, I suppose. But first we have to figure out what makes a golfer tick. Whatever it is, our dads have lost it."

"That's for sure," Penny agreed, pushing back from the table. "And we don't have much time. So let's get to work!"

•　　　•　　　•　　　•　　　•

The next afternoon, the two friends were ushered into the office of Myrtle Anderson, a prominent local family lawyer and Riverdale's perennial Women's Golf Champion.

As they entered the room, the tall, bespectacled attorney, seated at a desk littered with golf bric-a-brac, was staring intently at a computer screen, feverishly moving a mouse back and forth on the desk blotter. Before her sat a small sign reminding all who entered to "Keep Your Head Down and Your Eye on the Ball."

"Rats — I was robbed!" she blurted out, hurling the mouse onto the floor and kicking it as if it were something that had just crawled out of the wall.

"Oh, hello," she said sheepishly after her secretary announced Alison's and Penny's arrival. "I'm playing computer golf. Today, I'm taking on Pebble Beach. I'm two under after eleven."

After the Champion had collected herself, the pair explained their problem.

"An intervention sounds like a good idea," Anderson volunteered. "And relatively simple. You see, contrary to popular belief, avid golfers, far from being fanatics, are, deep down, rational human beings. Oh, every now and then a golfer may get a little . . . uh . . . carried away. But golf is fundamentally a mental game; it encourages logical thinking. All we have to do is confront your fathers with the reasons they should get back together, and they'll come around."

Penny found it difficult to suppress a giggle. "I'm sure you're a wonderful golfer, Mrs. Anderson," she said. "But I don't think you know our fathers very well . . . ."

"Nonsense!" the lawyer barked. "I know golfers much better than you, young lady, and they're all alike. Eventually, they'll listen to reason. And to prove the point, I'll be happy to help straighten them out."

Although Alison was convinced, Penny remained skeptical. The two agreed to seek a second opinion. They consulted Wendell McGill, a local real estate developer and past President of the Riverdale Men's Golf Association.

When they arrived at his office, the rotund, florid-faced McGill was bent over a golf ball, an unlit cigar dangling from his mouth, lining up a putt with a Styrofoam cup lying on its side some twenty feet away. As he brought his putter back, he suddenly noticed the two women standing in the doorway. Stroking self-consciously, he topped the ball, coming up five feet short.

"The magic is gone," he sighed. "I've lost the touch!"

After recovering his composure, McGill led the two to a worn-out leather sofa and listened to their story.

"Myrtle Anderson doesn't know the difference between a golfer and a sack of potatoes," he said when they had finished describing their dilemma. "Rational? The truth is we golfers—at least we *male* golfers--are ego-driven. That's why we keep coming back to the game like drunks to the bottle—to prove that we really can do it right.

"Your fathers obviously have lost their passion for the game. The only way to get them back on the links is to appeal to their self-esteem. Sometimes, golfers simply lose their self-confidence . . . ."

"But I don't think loss of self-confidence is the problem here," Alison interrupted.

McGill dismissed the suggestion with a wave of his hand. "Of course it is," he insisted. "Why else would a golfer give up the game? No, ladies, all we need to do is stroke your fathers' egos. And I'll be happy to get other Club members to help out."

Out of an abundance of caution, Penny decided to consult a local sports psychologist. She hadn't spoken ten words when the therapist interrupted her. "I'm afraid I can't help you, Ms. Greer. I stopped taking golf cases years ago: they're just too . . . uh . . . tough.

"Have you considered spiritual counseling?" he added with an audible chuckle.

"Well, what approach should we take—reason or ego—logic or self-esteem?" Alison asked after Penny had abruptly hung up with the psychologist.

"Why not try both?" Penny replied. "We'll start off by appealing to reason. If that doesn't work, we'll hammer away at their egos."

•   •   •   •   •

After a brief run-through with Myrtle Anderson and Wendell McGill, the intervention was set for the developer's office the following week. McGill invited Arthur by feigning interest in opening a brokerage account, Wally with a story that he was in the market for aluminum siding.

The tall, white-haired Arthur, arriving in a gray, three-piece pin-striped suit, was led into the conference room through the front door; the short, balding Wally, dressed in a Michigan State sweat shirt, dungarees and a New York Yankees baseball cap, was escorted in through a side entrance. When the two saw each other and ten others, including their daughters, in the room, they immediately tried to flee. McGill blocked their way with his hefty frame.

"Now, fellas," he said after Arthur and Wally, restrained by a phalanx of determined Riverdalers, had settled into uncomfortable straight-back chairs in the middle of the room, "I know this is a bit unorthodox, but we're doing it for your own good. Your fellow Club members — as well as your lovely daughters — want you to reconcile and start playing golf together again."

The two anxious-looking young women approached their fathers and gently took their hands. After a few half-hearted protests by the men, McGill, smirking, turned the floor over to Myrtle Anderson.

"Here are the reasons you should stop fighting and get back to playing golf!" she began matter-of-factly, pointing a three iron at the two antagonists like a no-nonsense home room teacher lecturing students in detention. "First of all, you've both blown this snowblower incident way out of proportion...."

"Baloney," Wally erupted. "That snowblower blew up in my face!"

"It didn't blow up," Arthur said haughtily. "It... uh... ignited. And if you'd been more careful...."

The attorney cleared her throat. "Be that as it may, gentlemen," she continued, "you two are natural golfing partners. Your games complement each other — you, Wally, with your strong play off the tee, and you, Arthur, with your skill around the greens...."

"That's ridiculous," Arthur interrupted. "Everyone knows I'm the backbone of our team. I've been carrying Wally for years."

"Oh, sure," Wally countered. "Like in the Two-Man Scramble back in '95, when I holed out of the sand in the playoff. You should be carrying my bag!"

The attorney's face turned crimson. "Well, dammit all," she exploded, slamming the club down on a nearby table, as if preparing to administer a thrashing to the two, "you've at least got to defend your Best Ball title. Ducking out would be positively . . . unmanly!"

Obviously alarmed at the direction the intervention was taking, McGill stepped forward, motioned Myrtle Anderson away from the men and hovered over the pair like an angry drill sergeant.

"Stop bickering, you two," he bellowed. "It's not getting us anywhere." Wally and Arthur fell silent.

Suddenly, a friendly smile crossed the developer's face. "Listen guys, you're the premier twosome at Riverdale. Whether in match play, medal play, alternate shot, scramble, skins, best ball, three-club—whatever—you're the team to beat. Around the Club, you're known as 'Mr. Ham and Mr. Egg.' You're . . . uh . . . legendary!"

Both men sat expressionless.

"Having said that," McGill continued, "just imagine what the members will say if you don't defend your title . . . ."

Before either could respond, a burly young man seated on a windowsill spoke up. "They'll say you chickened out–that's what they'll say!"

"Yeah," another agreed. "They'll say you choked. And would you blame them?"

Before long, others joined in the chorus of "support."

"There's no excuse for backing out of a title defense. What else would you expect people to think but that you're washed up?"

"Or that last year's victory was a fluke."

"Or maybe that you cheated."

"And everyone will call you names, like 'sandbaggers,' 'spoil sports,' 'cry babies,' 'bums' . . . ."

"Don't you ever wonder why no one else wants to play with you?" added Myrtle Anderson for good measure.

At this, the two guests got up, excused themselves and walked out, their distraught daughters following in their wake. The intervention was over.

•　　•　　•　　•　　•

"I was wondering when you ladies were going to drop by," said Ernie Evans as he puttered about behind the pro shop display case, restocking his inventory of golf supplies in preparation for Opening Day. "I assume you're here about your fathers."

"How did you know?" Penny asked, dragging a reluctant Alison up to the counter by the arm. "I didn't tell you when I called."

The lanky, white-haired pro, dressed in a bright red pullover and tan slacks, removed his rimless glasses, blew on the lenses and polished them on his shirt sleeve.

"Call it professional intuition,' he said. "Every spring, someone decides to give up golf, and some family member -usually a wife or daughter – asks me to change their minds. Since Arthur and Wally haven't signed up for this year's partners event, I figured that's what happened."

The two women recounted the snowblower incident for the pro.

"Sounds familiar," Evans said. "Golfing buddies have a fight, and then swear they'll never play with each other again. Usually happens during the winter, when their minds are on other things. They lose sight of what's important and what's not."

"But what can we do?" asked Alison. "We tried appealing to their essential qualities as golfers . . . ."

"Essential qualities as golfers!" Evans scoffed. "What essential qualities?"

Penny explained their efforts to tap into the heart and soul of the golfer.

"And there," interjected Evans, "is where you made your mistake. You assumed that all golfers are alike. Golfers are just as complicated as anyone else."

He paused and scratched his head. "But they do have one thing in common—something special that bonds them together."

The friends exchanged quizzical glances, then directed them at the pro.

"Tell me," Evans continued, "do your fathers collect golf memorabilia—you know, trophies, old clubs, stuff like that?"

Both women nodded. "Our rec room is filled with them," said Alison.

"And my Dad's den," said Penny.

"And do they read the sports pages in the morning?"

"It's the first thing Dad does when he gets to the office," replied Alison.

"And my Dad when he gets to the plant."

Evans rubbed his bony hands together. "Ladies, I think I've come up with a way to get your fathers back to fighting over their golf swings rather than over snowblowers. But," he added, glancing at the calendar on the wall, "we have to hurry!"

•　　•　　•　　•　　•

When the two men opened the sports section of the *River City Times* at work the next morning, a crudely-prepared black-and-white advertising insert tumbled onto their laps:

YARD SALE

Golf Memorabilia

Assorted Woods, Irons, Putters, Bags, Gloves, Umbrellas, Balls, Trophies, Cups, Medals, Plaques, Shoes, Tee-Shirts, Windbreakers, Ball-Retrievers, Tees, Ball Markers and Other Golf Treasures

Friday, April 6, 10 AM

134 Walnut Drive, River Grove

For information call:

15

Penny Greer   Alison Edwards

784-2201

Proceeds Will Be Donated to Charity

"What are you two doing?" bellowed Wally Greer as he scrambled out of his BMW in front of the girls' apartment building. On the lawn, beneath a banner announcing "GOLF ANTIQUE SALE—EVERYTHING MUST GO!", sat three folding tables overflowing with items of golf memorabilia. Moments later, Arthur's Volvo pulled into the driveway, coming to a screeching halt beside the makeshift outdoor bazaar.

"What does it look like we're doing?" Alison replied. "We're trying to get rid of this stuff."

"Like this piece of junk!" Penny explained, holding up a rusting putter with a tattered grip and a bent shaft.

"But that's the putter I used when Wally and I won the Partner's Alternate Shot Tournament in 1989," Arthur protested, grabbing it from Penny and clutching it fondly to his breast. "I sank a twenty-footer on eighteen to win with that so-called 'piece of junk.' It's priceless!"

"Well, what about these?" asked Alison, holding up a shoe box brimming with golf balls.

Wally suddenly turned red. "Why, those are balls I've used in all the tournaments we've won. I've always saved them—for   sentimental   reasons.   They're very . . . uh . . . valuable."

"They are?" scoffed Penny. "We'd be lucky to get five or ten cents apiece for them. Look, they're caked with mud, and have cuts, scratches and bruises all over them."

"Besides, what do you care?" added Alison. "You've given up golf."

"You can't sell them—and that's that!" Wally insisted, yanking the box out of the young woman's hands. "They're mine!"

"Yes," Arthur agreed. "All these things are . . . *ours*. They're our memories. They're irreplaceable"

"Well, you needn't worry," Penny said. "Do you see anyone else here? Does that tell you something?"

The two men looked at each other in embarrassed silence.

Within five minutes, Arthur and Wally were on the phone with Ernie Evans, signing up for the Best Ball tournament. Evans told them he had been holding a spot open for them, hoping they would change their minds. The two friends then called River Grove Equipment Supply and placed a joint order for a new snowblower.

"You know, Wally," Arthur said after hanging up. "I think we should take the rest of the day off and go out to the driving range to practice."

"Yeah, good idea," Wally replied. "You could use some work on your tee shots — they're awful."

"And you could work on your short game," Arthur countered, putting his arm around his partner's shoulders. "It stinks!"

THE EQUIPMENT

NEANDERTHAL

"Golf is a game in which you try to put a small ball in a small hole with implements singularly unsuited to the purpose."
                                                    Winston Churchill

"You begin to get the idea that maybe golf manufacturers are out of control when you find out they are making clubs and balls out of components used in nuclear weapons and bulletproof vests."
                        E.M. Swift, in McCord, The Quotable Golfer

To most in the upscale community of River Grove, Steve Harris was a man on the cutting edge. Founder of software giant Harris Systems Limited, the tall, gaunt bachelor lived in a solar-powered hillside home featuring state-of-the-art digital appliances, drove around town in a custom-made, all-electric vehicle designed and manufactured in Japan, and packed a hand-held computer from which he dispatched and received messages through cyberspace. A multi-millionaire by the age of thirty, the young self-made man had donated a wealth of computer hardware and software to local schools, libraries and charities. Twice voted "Visionary of the Year" by the National Business Computing Council, Harris was known in industry circles as "the computer guru's computer guru."

But, despite his high-tech reputation, around the Riverdale Golf and Country Club, Steve Harris was known by a less flattering title — "the Neanderthal Man."

"It's those golf clubs of his," explained Ernie Evans, the Club's lanky, white-haired pro. "They've got to be fifty years old, if they're a day."

In fact, Steve Harris's sticks were fifty-two years old, a vintage set of "Jimmy Demaret" woods and irons given him by his father when he was a teenager cutting his teeth on the ancient and honorable game of golf. Ignoring conventional wisdom that "modern" clubs, with their oversized heads, titanium faces, graphite shafts, larger "sweet spots" and other "forgiving" features (not to mention their astronomical price tags), were vastly superior to "traditional" implements, avid golfer Harris continued to use the steel-shafted relics well into adulthood.

"I like these clubs," he would say when asked about his outdated weaponry. "They just feel right."

And, for most, it was difficult to argue with success. Even with their worn-down surfaces and cuts, scratches and nicks, the decrepit clubs helped Riverdale's newest member quickly achieve a respectable twelve handicap on the Club's challenging eighteen-hole layout.

But, in the mind of long-time Riverdaler Mike Dagostino, owner of Dagostino's Downtown Discount Sports Super Store, Steve Harris was a dangerous heretic.

"Ernie, the guy's a menace. I mean, if other golfers started thinking the way he does, we'd be out of business!"

The veteran pro, stacking boxes of the latest model "ultra-distance" golf balls in the pro shop display case, shrugged off the warning. "Mike, those old clubs are just a personal quirk. They're like a worn-out pair of loafers you keep wearing because they're comfortable on your feet. Besides, Steve's in the software, not the golf equipment, business."

The burly, dark-haired Dagostino threw up his hands in frustration. "But that's the problem!" he protested. "Look, everybody thinks Harris knows all about modern technology—right? So they probably think he knows everything about high-tech golf clubs—and that he doesn't use them because there's something wrong with them. Soon, people will start taking their old clubs out of their basements and their attics. Business will dry up! It's bad enough competing against Sears and Walmart, without taking on my customers' grandparents, too!"

Dagostino's hostility boiled over after the local merchant—also a twelve handicapper—lost to Harris in the finals of the annual Men's Match Play Classic.

"You should be ashamed wielding those antiques," barked Dagostino, poking a meaty finger into his opponent's chest at a cocktail reception following the event. "You're an embarrassment to the Club."

Startled by Dagostino's upbraiding, Harris looked quizzically at his accuser as curious members gathered around the two to witness the confrontation. "What do you care what clubs I use?" he replied. "They're perfectly legal — and it's a free country."

"But you can hit straighter and farther with the latest models . . . ."

Ernie Evans, an experienced hand at mediating disputes among the exclusive club's often contentious members, stepped in to separate the two antagonists. "That's enough, Mike. Steve has every right to play those clubs. They're like old cars: perfectly okay to drive so long as they work. What's a 'clunker' for one is a 'classic' for another. Besides, golf has too many variables — from personal skill to weather conditions to what a player had for breakfast — to know whether the type — or even the age — of his clubs makes a real difference."

The pugnacious Dagostino refused to back off. "But everybody knows you play better with modern-day equipment. Now, maybe you can't prove it . . . ."

A sly smile suddenly crossed the software executive's thin face, like that of poker player about to lay a straight flush on the table. "The Golf Equalizer could prove it!" he said.

All eyes turned in his direction. "What the Sam Hill is the Golf Equalizer?" Dagostino sputtered.

Harris slowly removed his steel-framed glasses and polished them on his shirt sleeve. He cleared his throat, like a professor about to lecture a class of freshmen.

"The Golf Equalizer is a new computer program developed by Sportsman Software. It's a computerized golf game that eliminates the effect of individual differences on the outcome."

"Huh?" Dagostino grunted, as if Harris had just uttered something in tongues.

"It's simple. Basically, the Golf Equalizer employs computerized players. You just input the type of clubs they're using, and a handicap, and the computer does the rest. It plays all shots exactly as a typical golfer of that handicap would, whether good, bad or indifferent. The score is determined solely by the characteristics and quality of the clubs."

Silence descended upon the room, as if the young entrepreneur had just announced a cure for a dread disease.

"Sportsman Software developed the program for the United States Golf Association," Harris added. "They're already using it to test different brands of clubs. Being in the business and all, I'm surprised you haven't heard of it, Mike. There's a feature article about it in the most recent issue of *American Golfer* magazine. It's the talk of the industry."

Thus was a reluctant Mike Dagostino—unwilling to question modern sports science—goaded into pitting his "Python Powerball Extremes" against Harris's Jimmy Demarets in an eighteen-hole showdown on the Golf Equalizer.

"If your clubs win," Harris proposed, "I'll throw mine away and buy a new set at your store. If mine win, you'll post a sign on the clubhouse bulletin board admitting you were wrong—and apologizing to me."

•　　•　　•　　•　　•

It was standing-room-only when members gathered in the Club's main dining room the following Saturday to witness the highly-touted match. An air of eager anticipation filled the room as those in attendance argued over who would prevail and placed last-minute bets on the outcome of what had become known around the Club as "the Battle of the Bytes."

At the far end of the room, before rows of folding chairs, stood a small table on which sat a laptop computer, a projector and a pair of speakers. Behind the table was a screen, a wooden podium mounted with a microphone to one side. Not a single golf club or ball was anywhere to be seen at this test of modern cyber-sports.

As the audience milled about, Evans, Harris and Dagostino conversed with a short, professorial-looking man dressed in a green cardigan sweater and sporting a gray Van Dyke. Harris, nodding from time to time, was smiling confidently; Dagostino, a pained expression on his face, was fidgeting and sweating.

Evans approached the podium. "Okay, everybody, pipe down and take your seats," he said as the dining room doors were closed and the draperies drawn.

"I'll make this brief. Today's match will be conducted under the auspices of the United States Golf Association. We have with us Mr. Homer Winkler, the USGA's Regional Vice President for Equipment Standards, who will officiate the contest."

The bearded man took the podium. "Thanks, Ernie. The match this afternoon will be played on the Golf Equalizer Computer Program. Employing 'standardized' twelve-handicappers as our players, we have selected 'Jimmy Demaret' signature clubs for Player A (who will represent Mr. Harris) and "Python Powerball Extremes' for Player B (who will represent Mr. Dagostino). We've inputted over fifty characteristics of each brand—length, weight, shaft flexibility . . . ."

"What about age?" Dagostino interrupted gruffly. "Did you factor that in?"

"Age will be taken into account, Mr. Dagostino," Winkler replied with a frustrated sigh. "Now, I will launch all shots by clicking the computer mouse. The computer will take it from there. Are there any questions?"

There being none, Winkler booted up the laptop. Shortly, there materialized on the screen the graphic image of a male golfer, dressed in old-fashioned plus-fours and tam-o-shanter, standing on an elevated tee, confronting a rolling fairway lined with trees, criss-crossed by water and dotted with sand traps. In the distance, barely visible on an oval-shaped green, stood a small red flag flapping in a virtual breeze.

"*Number one is a straightaway, heavily-trapped, 378-yard par four*," intoned a deep voice, seemingly out of nowhere.

"What the . . . ?" Dagostino blurted out, furtively looking about the room for the source of the statement.

"It's the digital announcer, Mr. Dagostino," Winkler said, pointing to the laptop. "Just like on TV—except he's inside the computer."

"Oh," Dagostino muttered, smiling sheepishly. "Sorry."

After the announcer finished describing the hole, Winkler clicked on the mouse, launching Player A's drive. The audience gasped as they watched a tiny ball fly into the air, gradually descend and bound safely onto the fairway 220 yards from the tee. *"Great drive!"* crowed the announcer. *"Looks like this guy brought his 'A' game today!"*

Winkler clicked the mouse again, sending Player B's ball aloft. It flew well past Player A's drive, landing in a bunker. *"Too bad,"* the cyber voice taunted. *"Beached like a whale!"*

"Well, at least I out-drove him by thirty yards," a red-faced Dagostino said defensively in the computer's direction, as if whoever was inside could hear him.

A five iron by Player A landed four feet from the cup. Player B's eight iron barely escaped the water hazard in front of the green. *"Pitiful! Pi . . . ti . . . ful!"*

"It's the best I could do . . . I was buried in that sand," explained Dagostino to the ethereal voice.

"Quit making excuses and play," someone shouted from the audience.

Player B's third shot made the green, and from there he got down in two. Player A sank his putt for a birdie.

Both players parred the second hole and bogeyed the third. "Better hope your luck holds up," Dagostino warned Harris, rubbing his hands together in anticipation of the next hole. "I feel a memorable shot coming!"

"The fourth is a treacherous par three, two hundred yards long. To the left, a water hazard will swallow any ball hooked off the tee. To the right, white stakes denote out-of-bounds."

Winkler clicked. A four wood in hand, Player A launched a lofty shot directly at the green. Mid-way in flight, however, the ball suddenly veered toward the white markers.

"Hang in there," coaxed Harris.

As if hearing his plea, the ball came to rest in bounds. *"Close call!"*

Winkler clicked again. Player B's ball followed the same flight path. Overtaking the first ball, it landed out-of-bounds. *"Yuk!"*

"Damnation!" Dagostino exclaimed. "How come his ball stayed in and mine went out?"

Winkler smiled benignly. "It has to be the clubs," he explained. "Since the Pythons have a greater range than the Demarets, Player B's ball carried farther than Player A's. B's club made a bad shot even worse."

"Okay, okay," Dagostino replied irritably. "Just reload and see what happens!"

Once more Winkler launched a shot. This time Player B's ball flew low off the tee, then curved toward the hazard on the left. Dagostino grimaced as the sound of water splashing came over the speakers. "*P . ..e . . . .w! What a stinker!*"

Dagostino was apoplectic, as hoots and catcalls burst from the audience like buckshot. Even the staid Winkler was unable to suppress a chortle.

"What!" Dagostino huffed. "How come Player B screwed up again?"

Winkler shrugged. "Probably because he got upset and lost his concentration. The Golf Equalizer programs in such errors. And even the most up-to-date clubs can't protect a player against mental errors."

"Mental error, my foot!" Dagostino shouted, his face now crimson. "I never get upset--or make two mistakes in a row . . . ."

"What about the three shots you needed to get out of the trap on seven this morning?" someone called out.

"Or the two shots you hit out-of-bounds on twelve?" added another.

Dagostino, fists clenched, strode over to the computer, grabbed the extension cord and yanked the plug out of the floor socket. The screen went blank.

"There! That's what I think of your talking computer!"

"Mike, what are you doing?" said Ernie Evans, running over to the table and grabbing Dagostino by the arm.

"That thing's a fraud," Dagostino shouted. "Just because that program's high-tech doesn't mean it's right. I mean, everybody knows there's no such thing as a 'typical' golfer. Golf's a game of individuals . . . ."

Dagostino suddenly caught himself. "Uh . . . er . . . that thing's a fraud, and that's all I'm gonna say!"

With that, the sporting goods salesman stormed out of the room to a chorus of laughter and jeers. Evans shook his head, then declared Steve Harris the winner.

•   •   •   •   •

The following Saturday, the pro ran into the victor outside the cart shed. Harris had just come in off the course, and was busy cleaning his clubs with a towel. He was beaming. "Good round today, Steve?" Evans asked.

"My personal best. A seventy-three! And I owe it all to my new clubs."

Confused, the pro looked into Harris's bag to find a set of Python Powerball Extremes. "When did you get these babies?"

Harris smiled knowingly. "I bought them Monday at Dagostino's. Mike gave me a fifty percent discount."

Evans pursed his lips. "But why did you give up on your Demarets? I mean, you beat Mike on the Golf Equalizer . . . ."

Harris put his arm around the pro's shoulders and leaned close. "Don't tell a soul, Ernie," he whispered, looking around to see if anyone else was listening, "but after everybody left, Homer and I kept playing. It turned out that, on the seventh tee, Player A swung his driver so hard that he cracked the club head coming down on the ball—I guess because it was so old. Well, after that, the damn computer wouldn't let him use another club to hit off the par fours and fives, so all Player A's drives dribbled off the tee. He lost by seven strokes! I decided then and there to retire the Demarets."

Evans stared at Harris with his mouth agape. "You mean Mike only lost because he couldn't control his temper and walked out?"

"Right. But, having played with him before, I knew he had a short fuse and was easily frustrated, so I figured he'd probably give up. And that computer announcer can drive anyone crazy. Mike's only human, you know. Of course, I didn't tell him what had happened after he left. But I agreed that he didn't have to post that sign in the clubhouse. That's when he offered me the discount . . . ."

"You snake! But what did you do with your old clubs?"

Harris grinned like a little boy just offered an ice cream cone with two scoops. "That's the best part. I put them up for auction on the Internet, and some collector bid five thousand bucks for them. Can you believe that?"

Evans shook his head and smiled. "Ain't technology wonderful?" was all he could muster in response.

THE ACCESSORIES

PLANET GOLF

"There are now more golf clubs in the world than Gideon Bibles, more golf balls than missionaries and, if every golfer in the world, male and female, were laid end to end, I for one would leave them there."

Michael Parkinson, in Golf Talk

"What the Sam Hill . . . ?" roared Ernie Evans, peering incredulously out the pro shop window toward the members parking lot. "If those two think they're going to take that out onto the course, they've got another think coming!"

At that moment, looming in the distance like the spearhead of an invading army, appeared a motorized golf cart the size of an armored personnel carrier. Painted silver, green and gold, and covered with a red, white and blue striped canopy, the gigantic vehicle lumbered up the asphalt driveway at the head of a column of casually-clad golfers gazing up in awe. In the front seat, smiling and waving, sat Dan Crenshaw, his younger brother, Ralph, by his side. Overhead, flapping in the warm summer breeze, trailed a banner proclaiming "CRENSHAW BROTHERS DISCOUNT BROKERS — YOU GET WHAT YOU PAY FOR."

As the brothers emerged from the cart alongside the clubhouse, Evans grabbed the starter's microphone and shouted over the PA system: "Hey, you guys can't go out in that contraption. It's against the rules!"

Ignoring the pro, the duo quickly loaded their bags onto the cart, jumped back in and sped away like bandits fleeing the scene of a bank heist. Seething, the lanky, white-haired Evans stormed out of the pro shop after them.

This was not the first time the Crenshaws had crossed swords with Ernie Evans. Not known for their tact or impeccable manners, the heavy-set, dark-haired twosome made it a practice to regularly violate almost every rule of etiquette known to golf. They talked incessantly while others

30

were hitting; traipsed through bunkers without raking the sand; left ball marks on greens unrepaired; and gouged huge divots in the fairways without replacing them. And, to the chagrin of those forced to dodge their often errant shots, the word "Fore" did not appear to be in their otherwise colorful vocabularies.

Yet, whenever the pro caught them breaking a rule, violating a Club policy or simply making asses of themselves, someone on the Board of Directors would spring to their defense.

"I know we seem a bit lenient toward them, Ernie," explained Board member and perennial Women's Golf Champion, Myrtle Anderson. "But a lot of us have opened accounts with the Crenshaws since they joined the Club, and, with the market performing as well as it has . . . uh . . . we certainly wouldn't want to offend them!"

Cornering the pair at the first tee, Evans marched over to the cart and yanked the keys from the ignition.

"Hey, whaddaya doin'?" protested Dan Crenshaw, bumping up against Evans threateningly.

The normally unflappable pro poked a finger in the broker's chest. "What does it look like I'm doing? I'm putting you two out of business."

Ralph rushed to his brother's aid. "Hey, calm down, Ernie. We're just taking our new golf cart out for a spin. What's wrong with that?"

"You know damn well what's wrong with it," the pro retorted. "Members aren't allowed to take their own carts onto the golf course."

By this time, the small cadre who had followed the Crenshaws in from the parking lot had gathered around the tee box. They gawked at the garish vehicle like toddlers in a toy department at Christmastime.

"It's the latest in golf accessories from Planet Golf Incorporated," Ralph boasted to the curious onlookers. "The prototype of a fully-equipped, state-of-the art golf cart for the Twenty-First Century. It carries ten passengers and can reach speeds of up to fifty miles-per-hour. It features genuine leather seats, a retractable conference table, mobile phones, a portable TV, a laptop and a built-in mini-bar. We . . . I mean, they . . . call it 'the Execucart!'"

"How about a test drive?" someone suggested as the enraptured audience kicked tires, inspected the engine and examined the spacious interior of the vehicle.

"You see, Ernie?" Dan gloated. "Everyone wants to see this baby in action. Now, don't be a killjoy—give the people what they want!"

"I don't care what they want," Evans countered. "As long as I'm the pro around here, the rules will be enforced. Now, either you get a regulation cart from the cart shed, or else forget about going out."

The brothers decided to abandon their outing. "But this isn't the last you'll be hearing about this, Ernie!" warned Dan as they drove away. "The Board is going to be very interested in how you're stifling innovation."

"Innovation, my foot!" muttered the pro as he turned away and trudged back to the pro shop.

•   •   •   •   •

True to their word, the Crenshaws quickly petitioned the Board of Directors for permission to use the Execucart on the course.

"Our club professional is an anachronism!" declared Dan Crenshaw before a standing-room-only gathering at the next meeting of the Riverdale Board. "He's as out-of-date as hickory-shafted clubs and gutta-percha balls!"

Crenshaw's derisive reference to Ernie Evans was greeted with a burst of laughter from the audience, composed mostly of members of the Men's Golf Association there to support the brothers. Ross Griswald, the portly Chairman, called for order.

Dressed in a tailored pin-striped suit, complete with vest and suspenders, Crenshaw addressed the directors with the fervor of a banker recommending the launching of a hostile takeover.

"It's time to take our Club into the Information Age," he asserted. "Today, given the changes wrought by modern technology and telecommunications, the line that once existed between work and leisure has become blurred. More and more Americans—particularly busy professionals—demand the ability to work while they play, and to play while they work. And, ladies and gentlemen of the Board," he added, beads of perspiration now dotting his forehead, "Planet Golf Incorporated—the industry leader in developing and marketing innovative golf accessories—has, in the Execucart, created (if you'll pardon the pun) the perfect vehicle for them!"

Evans groaned as murmurs of "Tell It Like It Is" and "Right On!" swept the room.

"Yes," the speaker explained with a grandiloquent sweep of the arm, turning to face the audience, "Planet Golf has designed the golfer's workplace of the future. The Execucart permits him to play his beloved game while conducting business at the same time. In the Execucart, not only do you get around the course efficiently, but you can keep in touch with the office, stay plugged into the markets, even meet with prospects . . . er . . . I mean, clients. Planet Golf is revolutionizing the way golfers live and work . . . ."

"Just like Xerox did in the Sixties," ventured Myrtle Anderson, a self-satisfied smile on her face.

"And Microsoft and Intel in the Nineties," chimed in Ross Griswald, apparently not to be outdone.

"Exactly!" crowed a gloating Crenshaw.

Evans interrupted to point out that Riverdale's liability insurance covered only carts furnished by the Club. "That Execucart thing looks pretty dangerous to me," he said.

The Chairman scowled at Evans. "Don't be so negative, Ernie," he admonished the pro. "I'm sure we can find some way around a technicality like that!"

"Besides, my brother and I are good for it," Crenshaw assured the Board. "We'll indemnify the Club for any losses."

"Of course," he added, once again turning to face the audience, "there won't be any losses. *This is a sure thing!*"

After the Board voted to overrule the pro (even allowing the Crenshaws to house the Execucart at the Club, free of charge, to solve the insurance problem), Griswald confronted Evans in the lobby.

"I'm sorry, Ernie," he said, "but I think Dan had a good point about your living in the past. Things do change, you know — even the way we play golf."

The pro sighed. "Ross, the only way I know how to play golf is to keep your head down and your eye on the ball . . . ."

Griswald cut him off. "Ernie, the Board has made its decision. Now, we want you to cooperate and leave those guys alone. Understood?"

Evans simply nodded and walked away.

•   •   •   •   •

The Crenshaws soon took full advantage of their new privileges. Appearing every afternoon, after the close of the market, in the Execucart, the two quickly became the most popular members of the Club. Riverdalers vied for the privilege of accompanying them on the course, serving up "mulligans" and "gimmes" to the twosome, stretching the rules of golf in their favor, plying them with drinks after a round, all in the hope of currying favor with the brokers. Citing their busy schedules, the brothers would never play more than nine holes. However, this didn't discourage those seeking some insight into the market, some tidbit of inside information, some hot tip on a stock or even just the opportunity of hitching a ride on the Execucart, from lining up to play with them.

Meanwhile, Ernie Evans continued doing his job, puttering about the pro shop showing off the latest model clubs and balls, arranging tee times and pairings, and providing lessons to members. But, in spite of his efforts to immerse himself in the everyday details of being a golf professional, Evans couldn't help but feel that a sea change had occurred — that he no longer exercised the influence, or commanded the respect, he once did at Riverdale. One particularly slow afternoon he even found himself, pocket calculator in hand, computing the number of days remaining until his retirement.

Following Ross Griswald's instructions, the pro did his best to ignore the carryings-on of the brothers. He didn't object when they began handing out leaflets touting their daily "top ten" stock picks; nor when they installed a "squawkbox" on the Execucart over which they hyped such offers as a

"Two-for-One Investor Special" ("Buy $10,000 in mutual funds and get an IRA free for a year!") and "zero percent" financing on margin accounts. He didn't even complain when, blatantly ignoring the signs admonishing golfers to keep their carts on the cart paths, they seemed to go out of their way to ignore them, often taking circuitous routes to move from one hole to the next. "We never follow the beaten path," Ralph explained.

And when, one hot and sticky afternoon, the Execucart appeared flying a new banner exhorting members to "GET OUT YOUR CHECKBOOKS AND GET IN ON THE GROUND FLOOR!", Evans put it out of his mind until later, glancing out the window, he noticed play backing up on the eighth tee. The situation was explained when a beaming member drove up to the clubhouse and ran into the pro shop, excitedly waving what appeared to be a stock certificate in the air.

"Hey, Ernie, get yourself over to the eighth tee—pronto!" he said breathlessly.

"Is there some sort of trouble?"

"Just the opposite! The Crenshaw boys are holding a regular fire sale out there. They're offering stock in Planet Golf at only five bucks a share—first come, first served! Could be the biggest thing since color television!"

"More likely since the Edsel," the pro muttered under his breath.

Evans drove out to the eighth tee to investigate. There, he found the Execucart parked beside the tee box, surrounded by golfers listening in rapt attention while Dan Crenshaw, standing on the rear bumper like a peddler of patent medicine hawking wares from the back of a wagon, trumpeted the virtues of an investment in Planet Golf.

"And not only will Planet Golf manufacture and market the combination golf cart/mobile workplace of the future," he told his listeners, "it will offer a complete line of 'high-end' accessories catering to the needs of the upscale golfer. Already on the drawing board is a line of sportswear designed to meet the fashion requirements of both the golf course and the 'business casual' workplace, an adjustable club that can serve as a three iron on one shot and a sand wedge on the next, for the busy executive who travels light, a hand-held computer usable for everything from sending e-mail messages to gauging the distance to the flag stick . . . ."

As Dan harangued his listeners, Ralph, sitting in the front seat balancing an attache case on his lap, was busily accepting applications for shares and checks from those buying into the message.

"Now I've seen everything," the pro said.

"Want in on the action, old timer?" asked Ralph with a sneer, handing Evans an application form. "Never too late to turn your life around and make something of yourself."

Evans quickly glanced at the application, noting the address of Planet Golf as "c/o Crenshaw Brothers Discount Brokers, 128 Main Street, River Grove." He thrust it back at Ralph, then launched a large wad of spit into the air. "No thanks," he replied. "Too rich for my blood."

When, later in the day, the pro called Ross Griswald to complain about the Crenshaw's open-air boiler room, he was met with the same old argument — that what the brothers were doing represented "progress."

"As a matter of fact, Ernie," the Chairman added, "when I heard about the deal they were offering, I called Dan on my cell phone and put in an order for five thousand shares! Like they said — it's a sure thing."

Evans sighed. "If you say so, Ross," was all he could manage to say.

•   •   •   •   •

Before long, the entire Club had succumbed to Planet Golf fever. To induce members to invest in the fledgling venture, the Crenshaws began passing out free "samples" of new products to be offered the buying public by the manufacturer of the Execucart, including tee shirts, golf caps, balls, gloves, ball markers and tees imprinted with the Planet Golf logo (a dimpled golf ball encircled by Saturn-like rings); Planet Golf towels, mugs, pens, pencils and ashtrays; even a Planet Golf shoehorn that doubled as a divot repair tool.

In addition, with the blessing of Ross Griswald, the Crenshaws posted a chart in the clubhouse lobby tracking the daily price movement in shares of Planet Golf. Over the next few weeks, members watched the stock climb from five dollars to ten dollars to fifteen dollars a share and more. After it hit twenty (on the day Planet Golf announced its intention to establish "a virtual pro shop on the World Wide Web!"), the brothers mounted a more imposing chart (the top line at the dizzying level of $100 per share) to accommodate the runaway growth in the company's value. When a curious Ernie Evans, unable to obtain a quote for Planet Golf on his computer, inquired as to the source of the share prices, Ralph assured him they were provided by "insiders in the know."

"You've heard of the over-the-counter market, Ernie," he cackled. "Well, Planet Golf is traded under-the-table." Evans didn't bother to ask why the company didn't have a prospectus or even a corporate report available.

But the principal attraction remained the Execucart. After tapping out Club members, the Crenshaws began approaching outside investors, offering guided tours of the front nine in the oversized golf cart. Although Evans, citing the exclusion in the Club's liability insurance for injuries to non-members not "playing guests" of the Club or a member, Ross Griswald approved the tours.

"You're not being very creative, Ernie," he chided the pro. "Just give everyone a club and a ball before they go out, and suggest that they hit a shot or two while they're at it. That ought to keep the insurance company happy."

Yet Evans was anything but happy the following afternoon when, checking out a reported malfunction in the sprinkler system on the sixth hole, he spotted the Execucart, overflowing with passengers and under the control of Lester Little, a newly-hired sales representative of the Crenshaws, racing back and forth across the greenside bunker like a bulldozer in over-drive. For the old pro, it was like watching a gang of vandals defacing a cathedral with obscene graffiti.

"Mr. Griswald OK'd it!" the pencil-thin stockbroker squealed in protest as Evans dragged him from the cart before the horrified gaze of his charges. "How else can we demonstrate that this is an all-terrain vehicle?"

After placing a few phone calls that afternoon, Evans met with Ross Griswald to offer his resignation, effective at the end of the year.

"Maybe I am out of touch," he said with a note of frustration in his voice. "If this is a golf course I'm supposed to be running, it's sure not like any golf course I've ever seen. Anyway, there's an opening for a teaching pro over at River Grove Municipal . . . ."

In spite of Griswald's pleas, Evans refused to reconsider.

•　　　•　　　•　　　•　　　•

The accident occurred two weeks later. Lester Little, curious to see how the Execucart would perform on the course's narrow and treacherously hilly back nine, decided to ignore his boss's instructions and, at the helm of the vehicle, took his hapless charges that afternoon on a tour of the incoming holes. Soon thereafter, Ernie Evans received a frantic phone call in the pro shop.

"Mr. Evans, we're in trouble," came Little's high-pitched voice over the crackling static of a cell phone. "Come out to the fifteenth tee right away! And call 911!" In the background the pro could hear screams and shouts for help.

When he arrived on the scene, Evans discovered the Execucart lying precariously on its side, half-way down a hill, propped up only by a rotting tree stump and a dried-out clump of bushes. Little would later explain that he'd failed to negotiate the hairpin curve on the path leaving the fourteenth green, causing the overloaded cart to fly off the narrow roadway like a runaway roller coaster jumping its tracks, tumbling nearly twenty feet down the embankment, taking its terrified passengers with it. Spotting several occupants futilely struggling to extricate themselves from the wreck, the pro tried to bring order out of chaos.

"Just stay where you are," he shouted down to the distraught victims. "Help is on the way. We don't want to make a bad situation worse!"

For the first time in weeks, his advice was heeded. Soon, a Fire Department EMS unit arrived and began extracting the hapless passengers with ropes and cables.

"That thing's a menace," the shaken stockbroker complained as paramedics sheathed his head in bandages after pulling him from the crumpled wreckage. "It's too bulky to take tight corners, and the brakes don't hold on steep grades. It doesn't belong on a golf course!"

"So much for a sure thing," said Evans as he kicked away a plastic cocktail tumbler that had fallen off the golf cart for the Twenty-First Century before its final plunge.

After he'd made sure no one was seriously injured, Evans returned to the pro shop and called the Crenshaws. He wasn't surprised when the receptionist told him that the brothers had left the office and that she didn't know when they would return. When he called the next morning, he got a recorded message from the phone company informing him that their number was no longer in service.

• • • • •

"Well, Ernie, the Board certainly hopes this will induce you to stay around for a good, long time," said Ross Griswald as he signed the contract extending the pro's retirement date to his seventieth birthday and granting him a substantial raise. "When I told everyone you'd resigned, they said they'd have my head unless I got you to change your mind."

Evans laughed. "I confess that early retirement looked very attractive when the Crenshaws were still around . . . ."

Griswald winced at the mention of the name.

"God, I feel like such a fool," he confessed. "The only things missing were the ringmaster and the clowns!"

"Don't feel too bad, Ross. Those charlatans fooled a lot of people. Anyway, the State's Attorney's office thinks they'll catch up with them eventually. Con men like the Crenshaws always resurface: they just can't resist the temptation to — pardon the expression — take another sucker for a ride."

A weak smile crossed Griswald's careworn face. "Well, that's not going to make the members any happier about the special assessment to cover the liability for the accident — or the money they lost investing in Planet Golf. And, can you believe it, those deadbeats skipped town owing three months in back dues? Some visionaries!"

The pro scratched his head. "Well, Ross, you know what the French say about things changing . . . ."

The Chairman's face suddenly darkened. "Now hold your horses, Ernie," he said. "You may be right, but I'd rather not test that principle out on you. Just promise me you won't change. The members like you just the way you are!"

THE COURSE

THE BARRIER

"Golf teaches that the best courses are the ones that hardly change at all what God put there to begin with."
Marc Gellman and Tom Hartman, in Chicken Soup for the Golfer's Soul

"The duck hook, the banana slice, the topped dribble, the no-explode explosion shot, the arboreal ricochet, the sky ball, the majestic OB, the pondside scrupp-and-splash, the deep-grass squirt, the thin hit, the stubbed putt – what a wealth of mirth is to be had in an afternoon's witnessing of such varied miseries, all produced in a twinkling of an eye by the infallible laws of physics."
John Updike, Golf Dreams

Wendell McGill stood beside his golf cart, contemplating the grove of elms blocking his approach to the green. Spotting a narrow opening, he pulled a three iron from his bag, stepped up to his ball and set himself for his shot. But, as he took his stance, he hesitated: the gap he'd observed only moments before had somehow vanished. Frustrated, he walked back to the cart and yanked out a nine iron. He would, he decided, hit over the trees. Once more addressing the ball, he slowly brought his club back and checked himself again. The elms suddenly seemed taller than he'd remembered. Returning to the cart one more time, he extracted a seven iron. A punch shot, away from the trees, was definitely in order.

"Goddamn it, Wendell," his playing partner shouted, "make up your mind! You know that, whatever you do, you'll screw it up! Just get on with it."

An angry Wendell reverted to his original plan—a frontal assault. After all, everyone knows that trees are ninety percent air. That's a nine in ten chance of getting through. Striding confidently to his lie, three iron again in hand, he took his stance, looked up, looked down, waggled twice and swung hard. Following through, he heard the telltale sound of polyurethane colliding with wood. Instinctively he ducked, barely escaping a beaning by his ricocheting ball as it whizzed over his head.

Although all this transpired on a sunny Saturday in late spring, it could have taken place on any day that the fifty-something Wendell — President, CEO and sole stockholder of McGill Properties Limited — tackled the fourteenth hole at the Riverdale Golf and Country Club.

Wendell had not always done battle with the trees that bordered the long hole, jealously guarding its sharp dogleg right. For years, he'd played fourteen as if they weren't there, cutting the corner by driving his ball over them into the expansive fairway beyond. Few at Riverdale were capable of performing this feat.

But, as he'd grown older and flabbier — and the elms taller and thicker — the successful real estate developer increasingly found himself thwarted by the leafy barrier between tee and green. No longer capable of carrying the trees on the fly, he sought to outwit them. He tried hitting around them, past them, behind them and — sometimes — even through them. He used a driver, a three wood, a one iron and a two. He played "distance" balls, "precision" balls, "high-compression" balls and "low-compression" balls. Yet, no matter what he did, he usually ended up stymied.

"Wendell," his wife complained that evening after listening to his latest horror story, "if I hear one more peep out of you about those trees, I'm out of here!"

Wendell stirred uneasily in his chair. "I'm sorry, honey. I know I'm whining. But you're not a golfer — you just don't understand! I haven't parred that hole in over two years. I can't seem to make four to save my life! If only there were a way I could make those trees disappear...."

Dorothy McGill, her hands on her hips, stared at her squat, balding husband like an angry schoolteacher confronting a dull-witted pupil. "There is," she said. "Just do what you always do to trees that get in your way."

"What's that?" he asked innocently.

"Bulldoze them!" came the sharp reply.

An almost demonic smile crossed Wendell's pudgy face. He understood.

．　　．　　．　　．　　．

Around the community of River Grove, Wendell McGill was known as a man who got things done. Over the years, he had, almost single-handedly, transformed the once peaceful bedroom community into a sprawling suburban Mecca. Under his guidance, small mom-and-pop grocery stores had succumbed to giant supermarkets, independent retailers to national discount chains, cozy apartment houses to multistory condominium complexes, neighborhood movie theaters to mega-multiplexes and quaint village squares to mindless mini-malls. Wendell was a savvy developer, without peer.

But Wendell's reputation counted for little when he broached the subject of removing the trees bordering the fourteenth hole to the powers-that-be at Riverdale.

"Now why would we do something like that?" asked Ernie Evans when Wendell described his idea to the veteran pro. "Those trees give fourteen its character. Without them, it would be just another ho-hum hole!"

"We have lots of other projects on our plate," insisted Ross Griswald, the Chairman of the Club's Board of Directors. "Like re-landscaping the tees, adding drainage on the back nine and eradicating that pesky fungus that's been gobbling up the fourth green. Plus, there's no money budgeted for cutting down trees."

"Besides," added Board member and perennial Woman's Golf Champion, Myrtle Anderson, "why stick our necks out? You know how unpopular change is around here. Remember what happened last year when we added that pot bunker on nine? There are still members who refuse to speak to me!"

When Wendell protested that his proposal represented "progress," he was greeted by polite but stony silence. Rebuffed by the Club's elite, he decided to drop the matter.

But Wendell's change of heart did not survive his next encounter with the fourteenth hole.

"Use your head," Dorothy prodded her husband the following Saturday when he described in grim detail how his ball had come to rest against the exposed root of one of the elms. "You're not thinking straight!"

Wendell turned red. "You mean I should have taken an unplayable lie rather than trying to punch out?"

"Wendell, I'm not talking about your golf! I'm talking about the way you've given up on your idea. If you'd reacted that way twenty-five years ago when the Town Council balked at changing our zoning ordinances, we'd probably be living in a rundown shack today, without electricity or running water. Just do what you've always done in situations like this!"

Mystified, Wendell gazed blankly at his spouse. "Huh?"

The tall, angular redhead threw up her hands, collapsed into a sofa chair and emitted a dour moan. "Do I have to spell everything out for you? Here, I'll give you a hint—River Grove West!"

It took awhile, but it finally dawned on Wendell. Years before, when the Board of Education had scoffed at his idea of building a new high school on the west side of town, Wendell had spearheaded a community petition drive, arguing that the facility would cause property values to skyrocket. Hailed as a visionary by area homeowners, Wendell ultimately prevailed.

The next day he had his lawyer draft a petition to the Riverdale Board.

WHEREAS, golf is a dynamic, ever-changing game; and

WHEREAS, the members of the Riverdale Golf and Country Club are known for being in the vanguard of the sport; and

WHEREAS, the elms bordering the fourteenth fairway have become an eyesore, a safety hazard and a nuisance, and have long-since outlived their usefulness:

NOW, THEREFORE, the undersigned members of said Riverdale Golf and Country Club hereby petition the Board of Directors to remove said trees . . . .

Although Wendell's reasoning was, at best, suspect, he decided that, whatever it lacked in logic, the petition more than made up for in punch. After dictating a brief cover letter to his secretary ("please join me in this campaign for a better golf course and a better community"), Wendell instructed her to mail the petition to every member over 55 or with a handicap over 18.

•　　•　　•　　•　　•

The response to Wendell's petition was overwhelming. Unfortunately, it wasn't all positive.

When word of his plan got out, opposition forces mobilized. Led by Gloria Fritz, President of the Women's Golf Association, opponents of the scheme (a patchwork of preservationists, conservationists, environmentalists, nature lovers and low handicap golfers) circulated a counter petition lambasting what they called "McGill's Massacre."

> The elms on fourteen [their cover letter read] are part of the living history of the Club, a landmark every bit as significant as our Colonial clubhouse and our legendary observation tower. Not only do those magnificent trees add splendor to our championship layout, they form an irreplaceable part of the Riverdale ecosystem, critical to plant and animal life . . . .
>
> It should come as no surprise that the man behind this effort is none other than Wendell McGill — the developer responsible for paving over our beautiful community and converting it into a haven for superstores, superhighways and shopping centers . . . .

In the business world, Wendell usually bowled over the opposition with impunity. But now he reacted more with dismay than disdain. Although many older members joined an assortment of high handicappers and weekend golfers to support his petition, some of Wendell's best friends resisted, many shunning him altogether. Ted Hammer, a local attorney who'd teed off with Wendell every Sunday for almost fifteen years, suddenly switched to another foursome; Tom Belcher, President of the River Grove Community Center, who'd played low-stakes poker with Wendell in the Men's Locker Room Bar every Wednesday for a decade, inexplicably took the "pledge"; and Men's Champion Bill Davis, who'd always given Wendell tips on the practice tee on Saturday afternoons, began coaching his son's soccer team on weekends.

"What did you expect?" Dorothy chided when Wendell complained of friends abandoning him. "I mean, whenever you apply for a permit or variance, you get opposition. You should be used to it by now!"

Wendell idly stirred a cup of lukewarm coffee and sighed. "That's business, honey. This is . . . well . . . different. Isn't it?"

• • • • •

But no one at Riverdale was more troubled by the controversy than Ernie Evans. Although not in his contract, the lanky, white-haired pro had always served as unofficial mediator of disputes among members. Whether grappling with Saturday morning tee times for women, sanctions for slow play or banning "gimmes" in tournaments, he could invariably come up with a common-sense solution to problems satisfactory to everyone.

But the rhubarb over the trees had him stumped. Although opposed to Wendell's plan, he wanted to work out a compromise that would keep a lid on things. Unable to think of anything, he finally asked Gloria Fritz and Wendell to join him in the clubhouse snack bar for lunch one Thursday to hash things out.

Tension filled the air as the two protagonists sat stiffly at a table in the nearly deserted room, scanning their menus as if they had never seen the bill of fare before. Evans, taking a sip of water and clearing his throat, broke the ice.

"Now you two know why I asked you here. I want to get to the bottom of this thing and resolve it. What I want to know," he added, turning to Wendell, "is what's *really* bothering you."

Wendell, dressed in a blue blazer and gray slacks, tugged at his sleeves and fidgeted with his tie. "You know what's bothering me, Ernie," he replied, his voice cracking. "It's all in my petition. Those trees are old, ugly, dangerous . . . ."

"Wendell," Evans interrupted, "I asked what's really bothering you."

"What's bothering him," the feisty, gray-haired Gloria Fritz interjected, "is that he can't leave well enough alone. He sees something of natural beauty, and immediately he wants to tear it down . . . ."

Evans raised his hand to silence her.

The developer wiggled uncomfortably in his seat. Streams of sweat rolled down his cheeks. He felt like a prisoner of war undergoing interrogation by the enemy.

"Alright, Ernie," he finally said, mopping his face with a paper napkin. "The truth is I'm just not the golfer I used to be.

Back in the old days, I could carry those trees without thinking about them. I could par fourteen three out of every four times I played it. But now, I can't shoot par to save my life. Those damn trees make me feel old . . . like I can't cut it anymore!"

An understanding smile came to the pro's face. "Now we're making progress," he said.

He turned to Gloria. "Okay, what's bothering you? The truth!"

The President of the Women's Golf Association frowned. "Well, to be honest, a lot of us are sick and tired of Wendell getting his way around this town. We're so overdeveloped kids grow up thinking that strip malls, high-rise office buildings and detached parking garages are part of the natural landscape. For once, we'd like to see Wendell stopped!"

Sensing an imminent shouting match, Evans signaled "Time Out."

"Just what I suspected," he said. "This dispute has absolutely nothing to do with whether those trees belong there or not . . . ."

"Now hold on, Ernie," Gloria countered. "No matter what our motives, I don't see how Wendell can complain. Fourteen is not that difficult. Why, I par it all the time—and I'm a sixteen handicap!"

Wendell looked at the small, slender Gloria and laughed. "In your dreams!" he scoffed. "I'll bet that, if push came to shove, you couldn't par fourteen in . . . say, two out of three tries."

"I bet I could!"

The pro's eyes suddenly lit up. He reached into his back pocket and retrieved a blank scorecard. He suppressed a smile as he read it.

"Obviously, you're both risk-takers," he said. "Well, how far are you willing to go? Are you, Wendell, willing to drop your proposal if Gloria can do what she claims?"

Wendell nervously ran his fingers through what remained of his hair. He couldn't back down from his own challenge. "Uh . . . er . . . sure," he gulped.

"And, Gloria, will you drop your opposition to Wendell's proposal, and call off your supporters, if you can't?"

"Well, I guess I can try . . . ."

The old pro beamed. "It's all set, then. Be on the fourteenth tee tomorrow morning at eight o'clock sharp."

•   •   •   •   •

Friday dawned chilly and damp in River Grove. By seven-fifty-five, a blustery, rain-laden Northeast wind lashed out across the Riverdale eighteen as a hardy band left the clubhouse for the fourteenth hole. By the time the small caravan of golf carts arrived at the tee, everyone was soaking wet and in an ornery mood.

"What a shame!" Wendell taunted Gloria Fritz as he tossed a clump of wet grass into the air and watched it fly over his shoulders toward the back of the tee box. "The wind's against you. Makes the hole that much tougher."

"Pipe down, Wendell," barked Ross Griswald, who, along with Myrtle Anderson and Ernie Evans, accompanied the adversaries as official observers. "No mind games or trash-talking!"

The petite Gloria, dressed in a gray waterproof windbreaker and fisherman's hat, fought her way through the wind and rain to the elevated tee. For the first time, Wendell noticed that the red markers for women were ten yards behind the white markers for men. All the better, he thought.

"Here goes!" Gloria called out as she teed up her ball and took her stance. Unleashing a mighty swing, she sent her drive low along the left edge of the fairway, where it came to rest a hundred seventy yards out.

"Some drive," Wendell hooted. "You're still three hundred yards from the green—with trees in your way!"

But when the group arrived at her ball, Wendell was surprised to find that, by playing to the far side of the fairway, Gloria had left herself plenty of room to avoid the elms on her second shot. Wendell, who'd always challenged the trees on his drive, had never seen the hole from this perspective. Nevertheless, Gloria was so far away that making par seemed virtually impossible.

"What are you going to use now, Gloria," Wendell shouted through the whistling wind, "a rocket launcher?"

Ignoring his jibe, the grandmother of five confidently stroked a two iron into the teeth of the wind. Staying low to the ground, the ball split the center of the fairway, stopping about a hundred thirty-five yards from the green. When her third shot—a five iron—landed on the front apron, forty feet short of the hole, Wendell was certain he had one in his column.

"Not too late to give up," he said as she lined up her putt. "It would get us all back inside a lot sooner."

Gloria, a determined expression on her rain-splattered face, walked up to her ball, took her stance and stroked her putter firmly. Starting out to the right, kicking up a small spray of water as it rolled across the fringe, the ball hit the soggy putting surface running, quickly veering left, then back to the right. Looking for a moment as if it might drop, it suddenly encountered a puddle, slowed dramatically and came to rest a foot shy of the hole.

"Tough luck," Wendell clucked. "But I'll be a nice guy and give you that one."

Gloria looked at her rival quizzically. "If you insist," she replied, scooping up her ball with the head of her putter.

Wendell marched over to the pro. "Score one for me, Ernie," he said, beaming as if he had just won a stuffed animal at a carnival.

Suddenly, Gloria came storming over to the two men. "What do you mean, score one for you? I got a five—*a par!*"

Wendell looked at Evans like a little boy who's just been told that the circus has been canceled.

"She's right," Evans said matter-of-factly. "This hole is a par five for women. It's a par four only for men. But surely you knew that, Wendell. You've been a member here almost thirty years."

The developer's jaw dropped. "Uh...er...no—no, I didn't. I mean, my wife doesn't golf...and I've always played with other men—I've never thought about...uh...the women...."

Frustrated and tongue-tied, Wendell turned on Gloria Fritz. "You sandbagger! You tricked me!"

Wendell's opponent looked almost as shocked as he was. "You mean it's not a par five for everyone?" she asked the pro. "I always thought it was . . . ."

Just then, lightening flashed on the horizon. "Holy Moses," Evans blurted out, "a thunderstorm! Play suspended! Everyone back to the clubhouse — ASAP."

•　　•　　•　　•　　•

Back in the cart shed, waiting for the storm to pass over, Wendell and Gloria eyed each other suspiciously. In a corner, Ernie Evans conferred with Ross Griswald and Myrtle Anderson. Finally, the three officials broke up and approached the contestants.

"Okay," the pro began, "I think we've come up with something."

Wendell and Gloria looked at Evans skeptically.

"Now, there's obviously been a misunderstanding here — on both sides," the pro continued. "In fact, if you ask me, this whole controversy has been one big misunderstanding. But, be that as it may, rather than going on with this contest, we'd like to propose a compromise."

With that, Evans handed Wendell a soggy scorecard. "What's this, Ernie?" the developer asked.

"Just look at it, Wendell."

Peering at the card through watery eyes, Wendell noticed that, in the "Men's Par" column, the pro had crossed out the "4" appearing opposite the fourteenth hole and replaced it with a "5."

"What I'm proposing, Wendell, is that we keep the elms where they are, but move the men's tees back ten yards and change the par so that it's five for everyone. That way, you can play the hole like Gloria did just now, without feeling you have to challenge the trees. You can score par more often, just like you wanted!"

Wendell scratched his head. "Gee . . . ."

"And you, Gloria," Evans continued, "you'll get what you wanted — you will have stopped Wendell McGill!"

Gloria sighed. "Gosh . . . ."

"And, best of all," the pro concluded, pointing outside, "we won't have to go out there again."

Wendell looked at his nemesis and groaned. "I guess it is kind of nasty out," he said.

"I couldn't agree more," she replied.

•   •   •   •   •

"Well, Ernie, I birdied fourteen again," Wendell McGill crowed as he emerged from his golf cart. "That's three times in a row. Your idea of changing the par last year was absolutely brilliant. It's given me an entirely different outlook on the hole! I'm more relaxed and confident playing it. Even my wife is happy."

"Oh, it was nothing," the pro replied modestly.

"But, you know," the developer continued, "it's too bad none of us thought of it sooner. We could have avoided all that hassle—including the drenching we got that morning!"

"Maybe yes, maybe no," Evans said, smiling slyly.

Wendell shrugged. "Anyway, Ernie, one of these days I'll have another problem for you to solve."

"Oh! What's that?"

"In a few years," Wendell said, grinning, "I'll be so old and decrepit that I won't be able to hit my drives over the creek on twelve. When that happens, I'm going to propose that the Club fill it in with good, old-fashioned concrete. Now, twelve already is a par five. So, what are you going to do with that one, Mister Professional?"

Evans laughed. "Oh, that's easy," he replied. "I'll just do what I have to do."

The pro pulled Wendell's clubs down off the golf cart. "And, until then," he added, "I'm not going to worry about it!"

THE STAFF

THE RUB OF THE GREEN

"'Rub of the green' . . . . {W]hen a ball in motion is stopped or deflected by an outside agency . . . . Also, 'tough luck' or 'that's the way the ball bounces.'"

Encyclopedia of Golf

"I tell ya, Ernie, it's gone—vanished!" barked Ben Mitchell, leaning over the glass countertop, clutching a plastic cocktail tumbler in his meaty hand. "A twenty-five-hundred-dollar, special-edition, Byron Nelson signature putter—one of a kind—stolen right out of my bag!"

The old pro eyed the paunchy, florid-faced member skeptically. "Ben, how can you be so sure it was stolen? You could have left it out on the course. Or put it in your playing partner's bag by mistake. It happens all the time."

"Nonsense!" Mitchell grunted, taking a swig from his drink. "That putter never leaves my bag. It's an ornament—there just to impress people. I don't actually play golf with it."

The lanky, white-haired Evans scratched his head. "But who could have taken it? You store your bag here at the Club . . . ."

Mitchell motioned Evans closer, then glanced around the pro shop to make sure no one else was listening. "Frankly, Ernie, I think Hector Lopez swiped it," he whispered, his breath reeking of gin. "He's the only one who had access to it after the Member-Guest Tournament the other day!"

The pro abruptly pulled away, shaking his head emphatically. "No way Hector stole your putter. He's as honest as they come. We haven't had a single complaint about him since we hired him last year—not one!"

Mitchell shrugged, as if the evidence against the accused were overwhelming. "You can defend him all you want, Ernie, but that doesn't change the facts. Look, he not only had the opportunity to take that putter, he had a motive. I mean, how can someone like him support a family of six on the pittance he makes here?"

"He can't," Evans replied curtly. "That's why he holds down two jobs — the one here and one as a weekend bartender at Mario's. It's the only way he can make ends meet."

"That's his tough luck!" scoffed Mitchell, draining his drink and tossing the tumbler at an overflowing wastebasket. "Just the rub of the green."

"Well, as far as I'm concerned, Hector's done a damn good job overcoming some pretty tough breaks . . . ."

"Baloney! You can take a guy like that and spruce him up a little, give him a fancy title like 'Manager of Equipment Storage,' but he's still just a bag boy! And considering his background . . . ."

The pro picked up the discarded tumbler and placed it in the wastebasket. "That's ancient history, Ben."

"You know what they say about a zebra changing stripes," Mitchell countered. "Now, are you going to do something about this, or do I have to go to the Board?"

Evans raised his hand to calm the angry member. "Okay, okay, I'll talk to Hector first thing Monday. But I'm sure we'll find your precious putter somewhere."

Mitchell nodded and smiled. "That's more like it. Now, I have an important engagement in the Men's Locker Room Bar. Will you be joining me?"

The pro glanced at his watch. "At eleven in the morning? Try me after work."

"I'll be by," quipped Mitchell, plodding unsteadily out the door.

* * * * *

The following Tuesday afternoon, a glum-looking Ernie Evans sat with Hector Lopez in the clubhouse snack bar, pondering the mystery of the missing putter.

"I don't understand it, Ernie," said the short, dark-haired Lopez, idly picking at a chicken salad. "We've searched everywhere — the bag room, the locker room, the bar, all eighteen greens, even the swimming pool. It's disappeared!"

The pro took an unenthusiastic bite out of a club sandwich. "It's strange alright. I don't think we've lost a single golf club since you came on board. They always turn up somewhere—on the course, in the wrong bag, in someone's back seat . . . ."

Lopez shook his head and sighed. "I'm sorry, Ernie."

Evans reached over and patted his friend on the arm. "No need to apologize, Hector. It's not your fault."

Lopez smiled stiffly. "Just tell that to the members," he replied. "It seems Ben Mitchell's been talking. This morning, Mr. Jessups looked at me like I had some incurable disease. And Mr. Andrews wouldn't let me take his clubs off his cart. Said he'd keep them at home from now on. Reminds me of the old days . . . ."

"I think you're exaggerating, Hector. Most folks around here are willing to give a fellow the benefit of the doubt. Anyway, everybody knows Ben's just a self-important, loud-mouth drunk . . . ." As soon as the words had left him, Evans wished he could recall them.

Just then, the two were approached by Mike Dagostino. The burly member seemed startled by Lopez's presence in the snack bar.

"Oh . . . hello, Hector," he said, as if addressing an uninvited guest. "Ernie, you got a second? It's . . . uh . . . kinda personal," he added, furtively glancing at Lopez.

"Okay. Drop by in about five minutes."

When he returned to the pro shop, Evans found Dagostino standing in front of a display rack, fingering a long iron on sale.

"I didn't want to talk in front of Hector," the member said in a hushed tone. "After what Ben Mitchell told me . . . ."

"And just what did Ben Mitchell tell you?"

Dagostino hesitated. "That Hector stole his Byron Nelson putter . . . ."

"Oh, for Pete's sake . . . ."

"No, no, Ernie, just listen to me. This morning, to check things out, I asked Hector to bring my bag out from storage. And, waddaya know, my three iron was missing!"

"Now hold it right there, Mike," the pro interrupted. "Did you ask Hector what he knew about it?"

Dagostino looked quizzically at Evans. "Of course not! I didn't want him to know I was suspicious."

The pro groaned. "Great! That's a sure-fire way of 'checking things out!'"

"Come on, Ernie," Dagostino replied defensively. "All I know is that my three iron's gone."

Evans walked behind the counter, bent down and pulled up a golf club. "Is this it, by any chance?"

Dagostino's jaw dropped. "Uh . . . er . . . yes, it is. But where did you find it?"

"Right where you left it — sitting against the boundary fence on seventeen. Hector spotted it driving in this morning. I'm surprised somebody didn't steal it, out in the open like that!"

Dagostino grinned sheepishly. "I suppose, then, I shouldn't ask about Frank Thompson's ball retriever . . . ."

The pro once more reached under the counter. "I think you mean this," he said, holding the missing device aloft. "Hector found it lying next to the water hazard on eighteen. Frank must have knocked one in on Friday."

Dagostino chuckled weakly. "Well, you can't be too careful," he muttered as he gingerly shuffled out of the pro shop.

•　　　•　　　•　　　•　　　•

Evans was soon inundated with other reports of missing items — clubs, shoes, gloves, windbreakers, caps, umbrellas, watches — even a set of car keys. All turned up in some obvious place within a short period of time.

Then, complaints began to surface about Hector Lopez's "attitude." One member claimed the Manager of Equipment Storage had been unnecessarily slow in bringing her golf bag out one morning ("I'm sure he did it intentionally!" she insisted); another that Lopez had sneered at her when she'd asked for another golf cart ("he should know no one wants Cart 13," she fumed, "it's unlucky!"). Myrtle Anderson, Riverdale Board member and perennial Women's Golf Champion, even protested that she'd found specks of mud on her clubs after Lopez had told her he'd cleaned and polished them.

"He probably did it out of spite," she said. "I'm sure he's angry that some us have stopped tipping him—you know, since all the problems began around here."

Although such stories seemed exaggerated, if not downright unbelievable, the pro nevertheless confronted his colleague that afternoon in Lopez's cramped cubbyhole next to the bag storage room. Lopez was sitting with his feet up on a folding chair, listening to a Spanish-language station on the radio, gazing up at the photograph of his family he kept on the wall.

"You know, Ernie," he said. "We took that right after I got the job here. I put it up on the wall to remind me of the promise I made to myself after I got out of the half-way house—that I'd do everything I could to regain the trust and respect of my family and friends."

The pro smiled softly. "And you've done a pretty good job of it, if you ask me."

Lopez abruptly rose from his chair and turned off the radio. "But I tell you, Ernie, right now I'm this close to quitting!" he said, gesturing with his thumb and forefinger. "Ever since I got here, I've felt that all eyes were on me, that everyone was waiting for me to screw up—just for the chance to say 'I told you so.' Well, they got what they wanted."

The pro tried to mollify his friend. "Now, Hector, I admit this thing about Ben Mitchell's putter has gotten blown out of proportion, but the point is you didn't take it . . . ."

Lopez laughed bitterly. "What the hell difference does that make, Ernie? I've been accused of it. End of story. Things always break that way for me. And people never change. There's always someone who has it in for me!"

"Hector, you don't seriously believe . . . ."

Lopez waved Evans off. "I don't know what to believe! Anyway, maybe Mrs. Anderson is right. Maybe I do have a bad attitude. But I don't care anymore. The trust and respect of the members mean nothing to me if I can't trust and respect *them*."

For some reason, the veteran pro found himself at an uncharacteristic loss for words.

By the time the Riverdale Board next met, it seemed to Evans that, in the minds of most members, Lopez had been tried and convicted of the theft of Ben Mitchell's putter. He was, therefore, not surprised when Dennis Chaudaire, the General Manager, proposed that Riverdale reimburse Mitchell for his loss.

"Maybe we can get it back under our fidelity bond," Chaudaire suggested.

"But you can't do that unless Hector actually stole it," Evans interjected. "And you have no proof of that!"

The young General Manager looked at the pro condescendingly. "Take it easy, Ernie: don't let your relationship with this guy color your thinking. We all know how strongly you recommended that we take him on in the first place. The management went along, thinking we'd look good—PR-wise—reaching out and hiring someone like him—you know, sort of as a token gesture we could point to to impress the do-gooders around town. And we thought we could rely on him. After all, as far as we knew, he'd changed his ways."

"And he has, Dennis . . . ."

"That's not the point, Ernie. The point is that a lot of us don't feel we can trust him anymore."

The pro's face turned bright red. "But if you really believe Hector stole that putter, you've got to fire him."

Chaudaire smiled. "I doubt it's going to come to that. I'm pretty sure the situation will take care of itself. Given the way members feel, it's only a matter of time before Hector gets the message and decides to leave. Then our problems will be solved."

• • • • •

Within the week, Hector Lopez had resigned as Riverdale's Manager of Equipment Storage. In a hand-written note to Dennis Chaudaire, he said he'd be taking up bartending full-time, and thanked the Club for everything it had done for him during the year he'd worked there. The note didn't mention the putter incident.

Lopez never spoke to Ernie Evans about his decision. In fact, the pro only discovered that he'd left when, the next morning, he found his friend's cubbyhole empty, the photograph of his family taken down from the wall.

Later that week, while on his way to the exercise room, Evans spotted Ben Mitchell with a group of his buddies in the Men's Locker Room Bar, boisterously sharing a bottle of champaign. In his hand Mitchell held a battered old putter.

"Hey, Ernie," he shouted, hoisting the club into the air, "come join us in some bubbly. We're celebrating the return of my Byron Nelson putter!"

Although tempted to keep on walking, Evans stopped in the bar and asked Mitchell where he'd found the missing club.

"Funny," the member chuckled, slamming his glass on the bar for a refill. "Would you believe my Member-Guest partner had it all the time? You see, I was working off one monster hangover that morning, and didn't notice I had too many clubs in my bag when we left the cart shed. Strange how you can overlook things like that. Anyway, without so much as telling me, my partner took the putter out of my bag and put it in his on the first tee so we wouldn't be disqualified—and then forgot all about it! Guess we were having too good a time."

"Some guys have all the luck," the pro muttered.

"Rub of the green, Ernie!" Mitchell cackled, slapping the pro on the back. "Rub of the green. Of course," he added, "I'm going to return the $2,500 to the Club. And I suppose I ought to apologize to poor Hector. I tried to find him this morning, but he wasn't around . . . ."

The pro shook his head. "No, Ben, he's not around just now."

Mitchell shrugged indifferently. "Too bad. Well, if you happen to see him, tell him I'd like to buy him a drink!"

"I'll be sure to do that," Evans replied, walking away without looking back.

THE NEIGHBORS

GOLF ON TRIAL

"Consider a screaming long iron that rises and banks, fading or drawing exactly as we imagined, 210 yards to land precisely on target and stop within inches of the hole. From an eighth of a mile away! That is godlike . . . . Why quibble that this taste of perfection comes only once in a hundred shots, or once in a thousand? We taste the nectar once and must ever after continue to seek it."
    Steven Pressfield, The Legend of Bagger Vance

"Why does any man keep playing this damn game? It don't make no sense in the ordinary way of things. But, then again, this ain't ordinary. Game like this gets inside you, like a hook in a fish. You can wiggle all you want, but that hook ain't comin' loose. It ain't backin' out of your body once it buries itself in your gut."
Bo Links, Riverbank Tweed and Roadmap Jenkins: Tales from the Caddie Yard

A hush fell over the courtroom as a portly man in a rumpled blue blazer, white slacks and brown suede shoes approached the witness stand, turned to the clerk and, trembling noticeably, raised his right hand in the air.

"Do you solemnly swear to tell the truth, the whole truth and nothing but the truth, so help you God?"

"I do," he gulped.

Squeezing into the uncomfortable straight-backed chair, Ross Griswald looked out over the sea of spectators gathered that Friday in the hot, dimly-lit chamber. Awkwardly extracting a white handkerchief from his trouser pocket, he self-consciously wiped his brow, blew his nose and shifted about uneasily, like a condemned man attending his own execution. He watched as a familiar figure in a brown double-breasted suit strode up to him, grinning like a used car salesman about to nail a prospect.

"Good morning, Ross," the lawyer said. "Long time no see."

"Yeah," Griswald replied glumly.

Thus began the trial of Hammer versus The Riverdale Golf and Country Club (The Hon. Stanley A. Forken, Circuit Judge, Presiding). Once a prominent member of the exclusive country club, local attorney Theodore Hammer was now suing Riverdale, claiming its activities constituted a public nuisance.

The relationship between the parties had not always been adversarial. An avid golfer, Hammer had joined Riverdale as an up-and-coming young trial lawyer with a stable of well-heeled clients devoted to the sport. Twice Men's Golf Champion (it was said that no one was better from one hundred yards in), he had for years been active in the Club's affairs, serving a stint as Chairman of its Board of Directors, the position currently held by his lead-off witness, Ross Griswald.

At fifty, the slender, silver-haired bachelor had fulfilled a life-long dream by building a magnificent Spanish-style home on land bordering the twelfth hole, affording him an unobstructed view of the island green and the surrounding water. Moving his law office to the site, he was able to gaze upon his beloved links twenty-four hours a day.

Then Hammer met and fell in love with Nancy Oaks, an introspective young woman to whom he rapidly (and perhaps rashly) proposed marriage. A college English instructor with a passion for film noir, an aversion to outdoor sports and a rambunctious twelve-year-old son from a prior marriage, Nancy was appalled by the game's hold on her husband-to-be. As a condition to tying the knot, she made Hammer promise to give up his favorite pastime to spend more time with her and her boy Robbie, indoors, cultivating the finer things in life. Hammer reluctantly agreed.

But Nancy quickly learned that golf was a jealous mistress, not easily jilted. No sooner had she moved in with her new husband than she discovered that living in the greenside home was about as tranquil as occupying a pillbox in a battle-scarred no-man's land. Subject to daily bombardment by wayward golf balls, and forays by their frustrated owners, the Hammer residence proved to be a Hell-on-Earth for the new bride. Her sleep disrupted by sorties of Titleists and Slazengers, her studies interrupted by cannonades of Top

Flites and Pinnacles, her garden leveled by fusillades of Nikes and Wilsons, and her Sundays shattered by shouts of "INCOMING!" from Robbie who, perched atop the roof, would watch as battalions of weekend warriors advanced on the twelfth green, Nancy threatened to leave the lawyer unless the family moved to a more secure location. Unable to find a buyer for the place, Hammer, at his wife's insistence, finally did what any good lawyer in his position would have done: he sued.

•   •   •   •   •

"Now, Mr. Griswald," Ted Hammer, acting as his own attorney, began the questioning of the befuddled-looking Riverdale Chairman, "you understand that we are alleging that your golf course is a nuisance, do you not?"

"Uh . . . er . . . yes — I guess so. But that's a lot of bull . . . ."

"Just answer the question, Mr. Griswald," the lawyer chided, leaning over the railing and glaring at the witness like a no-nonsense drill sergeant instructing a cowering recruit. "No editorializing."

Griswald nodded meekly, and Hammer continued. "Now, as Chairman of the Board of Riverdale, are you familiar with the many complaints lodged by plaintiff over the past three months about golf balls raining onto the property adjacent to the twelfth green?"

"I am."

"Approximately how many such complaints have you received?"

Griswald's pudgy face turned bright red. "Darn it all, Ted, you should know that. You're the one who's suing . . . ."

Judge Forken, his bushy eyebrows bristling and his salt and pepper hair in disarray, looked down threateningly from the bench. "I admonish the witness to answer the question!" he thundered.

"Yes, your Honor," Griswald replied, wincing like a child threatened with a stiff thrashing. "We've received two hundred eighty-four . . . ."

Hammer scowled. "Remember, sir, that you are under oath."

At that moment, at the defendant's table, a scrawny young man with a pock-marked face cleared his throat. Thomas Trailer, the Club's lawyer (and Ross Griswald's son-in-law), signaled to the witness like a third-base coach giving a "hold up" sign to an over-anxious base runner.

"Oh, yes," Griswald corrected himself. "We've had two hundred ninety complaints. I forgot about the six we got yesterday."

Hammer, smiling coyly, folded his arms and began strutting back and forth before the witness box. "Two hundred ninety complaints, you say — in only three months. If my math is correct, that's over three a day . . . ."

"If you say so."

"And, Mr. Griswald, how much has plaintiff's damage claims — for cracked tiles, broken windows, shattered patio furniture, damaged plants and the like — cost the Club? In round numbers."

Griswald tugged at his shirt collar, as if a noose were being tightened around his neck. "In round numbers . . . about five thousand dollars. But that included a big picture window — a freak accident . . . and we are insured . . . ."

Hammer looked at the Judge, shaking his head, as if to say: "I rest my case, your Honor." He turned back to the witness.

"Two hundred ninety incidents — in only three months — causing some five thousand dollars in damage. Now, Mr. Griswald, I would call that a nuisance. Wouldn't you?"

Murmurs swept the courtroom. The judge gaveled for order. In the process, he ignored a half-hearted objection emanating from counsel for the defendant.

●　　　●　　　●　　　●　　　●

Ross Griswald stabbed idly at a plate of overcooked roast beef and cold mashed potatoes as he sat with Ernie Evans and Tom Trailer in the courthouse cafeteria during the luncheon recess. Tossing his fork onto his plate, he let out a prolonged groan.

"Ted really had us over a barrel," he said. "Did you see the look on the Judge's face when I said I wouldn't live in that house for all the tea in China?"

The young lawyer grimaced, as if he had just encountered a shard of glass in his tuna salad. "Don't remind me, Dad," he said. "You know what I told you about volunteering testimony . . . ."

"And you, Ernie," Griswald continued, ignoring his son-in-law and pointing his fork at the lanky, white-haired pro. "He sure put you through the wringer."

Evans shrugged. "I just told the truth."

The pro, called to testify as an "expert" witness on golf, had been forced by the wily lawyer to admit that modern-day equipment—oversized, metallic club heads, flexible alloy shafts, and souped-up, high-compression balls—while dramatically increasing the distance of the average golf shot, had done little, if anything, to improve its accuracy.

"In fact, Mr. Evans," Hammer had pressed him, fondling a titanium driver he pointed in the pro's direction like a rifle, "hasn't the technology built into equipment like this driver actually increased the peril to persons and property from errant golf shots, turning what used to be considered harmless miscues into potentially lethal misfires?"

Although protesting Hammer's characterization, Evans had agreed that the lawyer was, generally speaking, correct.

"But what I don't understand," Griswald complained, "is why Ted has so completely turned against the sport. I know it's a pain to have golf balls battering your roof and breaking your windows, but, until he married that woman, he never complained. He'd just send us a bill for the damage once a month. Now, he treats golf like it's the invention of the Devil."

Evans shook his head sadly. "I don't know, Ross. I've always believed that, once a golfer, always a golfer. Now, seeing Ted's hostility in the courtroom, I'm reconsidering."

"And imagine," Griswald continued, "asking the court to make us move the green a hundred yards from his property line. That would cost hundreds of thousands of dollars, not to mention destroying the symmetry of the course. It's outrageous!"

Just then, Hammer, carrying a small suitcase, his petite, dark-haired wife on his arm, approached the table.

"Good afternoon," he chimed. "Having a nice day everyone?"

Griswald yanked his napkin off his lap, crumpled it into a ball and threw it onto the table in disgust. "We were—until you showed up this morning!"

Chuckling, Hammer slapped Griswald on the back. "Good one, Ross. But at least now you appreciate how it feels to be subjected to daily bombardment—like Nancy and I are!"

"And it serves you right, if you ask me," Nancy Hammer huffed, her nose in the air. "Golf is such a silly game. Grown men and women in Bermuda shorts and funny hats swatting little white balls around like children. It's undignified!"

"Of course," Hammer said, "our settlement offer still stands. Buy us out for half a million dollars and we'll drop the lawsuit and be out of your lives forever!"

"Ridiculous!" replied Griswald, rising from the table abruptly. "That's nearly twice the value of your place . . . ."

Evans, trying to ward off further bickering, asked Hammer the time. The lawyer glanced at his watch. "Time to kick some butt," he cackled. "And time for you to get to the airport," he said to his wife, whisking her away from the table.

•   •   •   •   •

That afternoon, Hammer continued his assault on Riverdale by addressing the court.

"Your Honor," he began in the most solemn, lawyerly tone, "as you know, the laws of this state define a 'nuisance' as 'a use of property or a course of conduct that substantially interferes with the legal rights of others by causing damage, annoyance or inconvenience.' Plaintiff believes this morning's testimony amply demonstrates that defendant's golf course fits this definition to a tee (if you'll pardon the expression).

"But, in everyday parlance, a 'nuisance' can also be any activity that is noxious, vexatious or bothersome, whether or not interfering with others. And, this afternoon, I intend to prove that golf at Riverdale meets this definition as well. Therefore, I call to the stand Mr. Horace Stapley . . . ."

With that, Tom Trailer shot up out of his seat like a slice of burnt rye bread popping out of a toaster. "Objection, your Honor," he pleaded. "This is irrelevant, immaterial . . . ."

"Sit down, Mr. Trailer!" the Judge ordered. "This is a court of equity. There's no jury here. I'll allow the evidence."

There followed a parade of the lame, the halt and the blind, as a legion of witnesses testified how golf had ruined their lives. Stapley, speaking from a wheelchair, told the court how, playing at Riverdale as a guest, he had broken his back falling forty feet off a rocky ledge trying to retrieve a ball hit out of bounds. William Hatten, a rotund, florid-faced man making his way to the stand with the aid of a walker, testified how he had to give up golf after suffering a stroke on the Riverdale course playing in one hundred degree heat. Florence Normand, widow of late Riverdale member Peter, tearfully recounted how she and her husband had been forced into bankruptcy when his passion for two-dollar Nassau became an obsession with gambling, "including," she sobbed, "five hundred dollar greenies and thousand dollar skins." After each witness stepped down, Hammer would, over Trailer's futile objection, shake his head and mutter: "And they claim this isn't a nuisance!"

Ross Griswald spent the afternoon with his head buried in his hands, while his son-in-law took copious notes, none of which seemed to assist him in conducting an effective cross-examination. Ernie Evans, on the other hand, spent most of his time pondering how the attitude of so avid a golfer as Ted Hammer could have changed so drastically in so short a period of time.

•   •   •   •   •

Arriving at the pro shop early the next morning, Evans was greeted by George Martinez, the Course Superintendent.

"Ernie, there's something funny going on out at the twelfth green," Martinez said, a puzzled expression on his face. "I've never seen anything like it!"

"Something funny? What?"

"You gotta see for yourself."

Within five minutes, the two were standing on the twelfth green, peering down at the putting surface like detectives scouring the scene of a crime.

"I'll be," Evans said as he examined a series of tiny depressions near the hole. "Someone—or something—really did a job on this! Have you noticed this before?"

Martinez looked away for a moment, as if embarrassed to answer. "Well, to tell you the truth, something like this showed up out here about two weeks ago. But I had other things on my mind that day, so I didn't follow up. And the grass ultimately grew back, and whatever it was disappeared . . . ."

"That's okay, George. We're following up now."

The pro got down on his knees for a closer look at the mysterious craters. "What do you think they are?"

"They can't be ball marks," Martinez said. "Look, there are at least twenty-five of them, all within three paces of the flag stick. Our members just aren't that accurate. Plus," he added, "they weren't there yesterday afternoon when I checked the green before going home."

"Do you think they could be animal tracks?"

Martinez rubbed his chin thoughtfully. "I don't think so. We do get deer around here at night. But they don't wear tennis shoes," he said, pointing to a trail of small telltale footprints on the putting surface.

"And neither do our players," Evans replied. "But how do you think they got here, then?"

Martinez arched his eyebrows. "My guess is it's that Mr. Hammer. He's had it in for us ever since he quit the Club. I think he put something in the soil . . . poison or something."

Back at the clubhouse, Evans had a phone message from Ross Griswald.

"Ernie," Griswald growled when the pro returned the call, "I've been talking it over with Tom, and I've decided to recommend to the Board that we take Ted up on his settlement offer. He's really got us behind the eight-ball. Besides, Tom found out that Judge Forken is a rabid tennis nut who's never picked up a golf club in his life. We're sunk."

The pro protested. "Ross, I think I may be onto something that will help us out. I can't tell you what it is at this point—and it may be just a red herring—but give me the rest of the weekend to pursue it. It could mean the difference between victory and defeat."

"Okay, Ernie, you have until five o'clock tomorrow!"

•   •   •   •   •

That evening, as the sun was setting over River Grove, Ernie Evans hopped into a golf cart and drove out to the twelfth green. Positioning himself in the bushes on the far side of the water hazard, he waited in silence to see whether his hunch would pan out.

As a full moon rose in the sky, Evans watched the animal life of Riverdale reveal itself, emerging from the cover of shrubbery and trees to roam the fairways and greens. Squirrels and chipmunks cautiously ventured out onto the newly-mown grass in search of food, while neighborhood dogs and cats playfully romped on the fairway far from the view of their masters. A family of deer approached the green from out of the shadows, but turned back when they reached the water hazard, apparently finding the barrier impassable. Meanwhile, Evans, swatting mosquitoes and dodging bees in the muggy summer evening air, concluded that, if not a nuisance to players or the neighbors, golf certainly was a nuisance to a head pro.

Dozing off, the pro was suddenly aroused around nine-thirty by a blinding flash of light from across the way. He lifted himself onto his haunches and, rubbing his eyes, gazed out at the green, now illuminated by the beams of three giant floodlights positioned atop the roof of the Hammer residence.

Within seconds, Evans heard a cracking sound in the distance, and then a "thunk" emanating from the direction of the green.

Craning his neck to see over the bushes, he spotted a solitary golf ball rolling on the putting surface toward the flag. This was followed by another "thunk," and yet another, each announcing a ball landing on the green within ten feet of the hole.

"Great shot, Dad," he heard a young boy's voice call out.

"Aw, that was nothing, son," came the reply. "I can do that with my eyes closed. All it takes is a little practice. Now, you try."

There followed the sound of a club striking a ball, a splash, a circle of ripples in the moonlit water and a high-pitched cry of "Oh, no!"

•   •   •   •   •

"You caught me red-handed, Ernie," Ted Hammer admitted as he handed the pro a glass of lemonade in his memento-laden den. "I'm the guy responsible for tearing up the twelfth green. I've been chipping golf balls at night when my wife's been away. The truth is that I just can't seem to get golf out of my blood."

He turned to Robbie and gave the dark, slender boy a gentle pat on the shoulder. "And I didn't want the kid here growing up without learning what a great game it is."

Hammer paused, then chuckled to himself. "Of course, he needs a few lessons — particularly in repairing ball marks!"

Evans, examining the treasure trove of golf bric-a-brac Hammer kept in a display case along the wall, smiled softly and shrugged. "I'm not surprised. I kinda figured it was you shooting balls onto the green. Who else could hit so many so close to the hole? Anyway, when I saw you practically caressing that golf club in the courtroom yesterday, and that watch you were wearing in the cafeteria — that dirt-cheap prize you won for finishing fifth in last year's Labor Day Classic — I knew all your anti-golf rhetoric was just an act."

Hammer glanced at his time piece, a look of guilt on his face. "Yeah, only a confirmed golfer would wear something this tacky .... And, of course, lawyers will be lawyers."

"But, if you love the game so much, why did you put us all through this? Couldn't you have worked something out with Nancy?"

Hammer looked up to the heavens as if for guidance. "Who knows why love makes a man do what he does?" he sighed philosophically. "Maybe, at the end of the day, I really wanted to lose. I was scared to death that Ross would accept that ridiculous settlement offer of mine. Of course, if I'd gotten you to move the green back a hundred yards, I could have taken full wedge shots from the back lawn. . ."

The pro scowled.

"Anyway, I hope I haven't made too much of a . . . er . . . nuisance of myself," Hammer added.

•   •   •   •   •

The case of Hammer versus The Riverdale Golf and Country Club was settled amicably before the opening of court the following Monday. In exchange for the dropping of his lawsuit, the Club agreed to reinstate Ted Hammer to full membership, without payment of any additional initiation fee.

Nancy Hammer, her protesting son in tow, promptly left her husband, moving to a new apartment complex on campus, miles from the nearest golf course. However, a young man eerily resembling Robbie, his eyes hidden beneath dark glasses, can often be seen, after school hours, on the practice tee at Riverdale, hitting balls beside Ted Hammer.

People say the kid's a natural.

THE TECHNIQUE

THE SLUMP

"When you turn in a medal score of a hundred and eight on two successive days, you get to know something about Life."
P. G. Wodehouse, *"Golfing Tigers and Literary Lions"*

"He comes to realize that the game is not against the foe, but against himself. His little self. That yammering fearful ever-resistant self that freezes, chokes, tops, nobbles, shanks, skulls, duffs, flubs. This is the self we must defeat."
Steven Pressfield, *The Legend of Bagger Vance*

"Ernie, what are you doing to me?" moaned Mike Dagostino as he read the tournament pairings posted on the pro shop bulletin board. "You've teamed me with Jack Frawley again. He and I played together last month!"

Ernie Evans, stacking boxes of golf balls in the display case, eyed Dagostino suspiciously. "You want another partner?" the pro asked. "I thought you two were friends."

"We are—sort of," Dagostino stammered, averting his eyes like a child caught in a lie. "It's just that ... oh, you know ...."

"No, I don't know. Tell me."

Dagostino groaned. "It's ... it's just that Jack hasn't been playing very well lately ...."

"Why should you care? That's all reflected in his handicap. And it's only a temporary slump."

"Temporary slump! You call three straight months of lousy golf a temporary slump? I call it a ... a ... a *disease*!"

The lanky, white-haired pro shook his head in frustration. "You wouldn't be worried that he's contagious, now would you, Mike?"

The burly Dagostino balked at the suggestion. "Of course not!" he insisted. "I'm not superstitious—like some people around here . . . ."

Rather than arguing further, Evans cut the conversation short. "Okay, I'll see what I can do."

But finding another partner for Jack Frawley would not be easy. Once one of the most popular members of the Riverdale Golf and Country Club, the young, sandy-haired insurance salesman was now a virtual pariah, shunned by fellow golfers after lapsing into what seemed to be a permanent golfing coma.

It all began one Sunday when Jack, golfing with his regular foursome, played an eight iron on a routine approach to fifteen. Swinging easily, he made contact with the ball, then watched in horror as it flew, not toward its intended target, but at almost a right angle to the green.

"Holy Moses!" he cried, doffing his cap and scratching his head. "What was that?"

"I don't know," muttered one of his buddies, nervously backing away. "But, whatever it was, it wasn't pretty."

Soon, Jack was duffing the simplest of shots—hooking drives, slicing irons, chunking chips, yanking putts. Eventually, he was exhibiting the full-blown symptoms of a golfer in a slump: the tight throat and sweaty palms as he took his stance, the numbness in his hands and arms as he made contact with the ball, and the sinking sensation he felt as he watched his shot take off on its errant trajectory. For years a respectable twelve, Jack's handicap soared to a horrendous twenty-three.

Jack's playing partners, fearing his condition infectious, took to standing ten or twenty paces behind him when he addressed his ball, averting their eyes as he swung. Stories soon circulated of other members experiencing similar problems after playing with Jack. Ultimately, many of his regular partners began canceling matches or turning down his invitations to play. He was being quarantined.

●　　　●　　　●　　　●　　　●

Not only an avid golfer, but a compulsive extrovert as well, newly-wed Jack soon became desperate. Like any good Riverdaler, he sought the advice of Ernie Evans, the resident graybeard.

"Ernie, you've got to help me!" he pleaded to the pro one morning. "This . . . this slump . . . is ruining my life. It's all I think about, day and night! My wife says, if I don't stop moping around, she'll throw me out of the house!"

"Calm down, Jack," the pro replied, opening a dusty and dog-eared copy of the *Encyclopedia of Golf*. "Let's see," he mumbled thoughtfully, running a finger down the index page. "Slump. Well, there's information here . . . on sculling . . . on shanking . . . and on slicing — I guess you're doing all of that, eh? But there's nothing listed for slumping!"

"Get serious, Ernie," Jack protested. "This is my golf game we're talking about!"

Chuckling good-naturedly, the pro put his arm around Jack's shoulders. "Alright, let's take a look," he said with the air of a country doctor cajoling an anxious patient to say "Ahh."

Taking Jack to the practice tee, Evans had him hit shots for almost thirty minutes, using every club in his bag. Each time, the ball flew straight and true toward its intended target. On the putting green, Jack achieved similarly flawless results, even draining a winding putt of some fifty feet.

"I don't understand," Jack finally said, slamming his putter back into his bag. "When I'm on the course, I botch every second or third shot. But, when I'm practicing, nothing bad happens."

Evans sighed. "It's a mystery alright. But then there are only two things certain about a slump. The first is that it has a will of its own: you can't control it."

Jack frowned. "Wonderful! What's the second?"

Evans smiled benignly. "The second is that it's like the common cold — no matter how bad it gets, eventually it goes away!"

Jack shook his head and sighed. "Is that all you can tell me, Ernie — that eventually it will go away?"

Evans patted his pupil on the back. "Sorry I can't be more helpful. But take heart—you won't suffer from this forever. And, don't forget, golf's only a game."

•   •   •   •   •

The promise of eventual recovery did not satisfy Jack. He sought a second opinion—not from another pro, but from a collection of instructional videos he purchased at fellow Riverdaler Mike Dagostino's Downtown Discount Sports Super Store, including "The Duffer's Guide to Golfing Gaffs" and "Golf Techniques for Dummies." The next day, however, an angry Jack called Dagostino demanding his money back.

"These tapes don't help a bit!" he complained. "Oh, they're okay if something's wrong with your game. But they're useless when *everything's* wrong!"

Convincing himself that his problem was mental, Jack next consulted Dr. Delbert Jenkins, a local sports psychologist. Dr. Jenkins, a short, bearded man who clearly had never lifted a golf club in his life, listened in stony silence as Jack, sinking into an uncomfortable divan in his stuffy, dimly-lit office, rambled on for almost an hour about his deteriorating play.

"Well, Mr. Frawley," the doctor opined as he handed Jack his statement for $250, "it strikes me you have two alternatives. One is to give up golf altogether. The other is to undergo months—perhaps years—of therapy. By the way, does your insurance cover mental illness?"

Jack decided the good doctor was a quack.

"You've been taken over by some demon," Jack's new bride railed that evening after enduring yet another dinner-table monologue about "the thing." "Some supernatural force has a hold on you."

Taking her literally, Jack was on the telephone the next day with a psychic named Veronica, whose 1-900 number he'd seen on a TV infomercial for the "Occult Friends Network."

"You've been unlucky in love," the husky-voiced Veronica intoned after Jack revealed his wife's unsympathetic attitude.

"No—you don't understand," Jack insisted. "I've been unlucky in golf—*in golf!*"

"You're in denial," the seer replied. "Deep down, you're problem is one of relationships . . . ."

Jack hung up before his ten toll-free minutes were up.

Meanwhile, Ernie Evans's conscience bothered him. Although certain his advice had been correct, and that Jack's problem would ultimately go away, he worried that perhaps he'd been a bit insensitive. He knew that, no matter how many times he'd remind someone with a hitch in his back swing or a yank in her follow-through that golf was only a game, any dedicated player—whether weekend duffer or scratch golfer—approached the sport with utter seriousness.

One afternoon, pondering what to do, Evans ran into Joyce Jameson, Riverdale's Coordinator of Special Events.

"How's our pet project coming along, Ernie?" she asked.

Momentarily confused, Evans finally realized what she was referring to. "Oh, sure—our project. Well, I've had problems recruiting members to help . . . ."

At that moment, the pro knew what he had to do.

•   •   •   •   •

When he arrived at the clubhouse the following afternoon, Jack was in a foul mood. After a trying morning in the office, he'd received a call from Ernie Evans asking to meet him on the practice tee at two.

"I've got some . . . uh . . . fellow golfers I'd like you to meet," Evans had said. "They might be able to help."

As he descended the cart path to the driving range, Jack was surprised to find the pro surrounded by a group of children, excitedly jumping up and down, clamoring for his attention like famished playgrounders mobbing an ice cream vendor. "Let *me* hit the ball! Let *me* hit the ball!"

"Oh, there you are," Evans said as he spotted Jack coming down the hill. "I want to introduce you to some new friends of mine."

Speechless, Jack led Evans aside, out of the hearing of the children.

"Ernie, if this is a joke, it's in pretty poor taste. My game may have gone into the dumpster, but suggesting I play with kids . . . ."

The pro looked surprised. "Hey, you've got it all wrong. I'm not asking you to play with them. I'm asking you to *help* them."

Jack gazed blankly at the pro. "Huh?"

"You see," Evans continued, "these youngsters are part of something called Operation Good Time. It's a charity devoted to giving city kids the opportunity to participate in sports, like golf and tennis, that they wouldn't otherwise be exposed to. The Club's agreed to help this summer by letting them come out and use the driving range twice a week under adult supervision. When they're old enough, we'll let them onto the course. It's a great program."

Jack's face suddenly turned bright red. "Gee, I'm sorry, Ernie. I assumed you asked me here to deal with my problems . . . ."

"In a way, I did. Anyway, can you help us out on Tuesday and Thursday afternoons?"

Jack's jaw dropped. "Are you asking me to give golf lessons—the way I've been playing?"

The pro smiled. "You bet I am. Look, you haven't been duffing shots on the practice tee. Besides, these kids don't care about your slump. All they want is a grown-up to give them guidance and support. And they're clearly more than I can handle by myself."

Jack couldn't resist the pro's logic, particularly after he was encircled by the horde of wide-eyed nine to eleven year-olds, all asking for his help. For the next hour, pacing back and forth behind the diminutive golfers like a gruff instructor at a rifle range, he watched them hook, slice, top and hack shots off the practice tee. Although it wasn't pretty, Jack was enthusiastic. "Place your feet a little farther apart, Linda, and keep your eye on the ball." "Don't grip the club so tightly, Joey." "Keep your head down, Hector, and make sure to follow through." "Great shot, Ellen—couldn't have done better myself!"

By the end of the afternoon, Jack was totally immersed in helping the youngsters. And not one of them mentioned his slump.

• • • • •

"I just wanted to thank you, Ernie," Jack said, popping into the pro shop a few weeks later on his way to the first tee. "You were absolutely right. I've broken out of my slump; I'm hitting 'em like I used to. And people are playing with me again. I'm back!"

"Congratulations, Jack," the pro replied. "But, you know, we sometimes blow things out of proportion. Slumps are never as serious--or as important—as they sometimes seem. Anyway, now that you're here, I want to thank *you* for helping out with Operation Good Time. The kids really appreciate everything you're doing."

Jack laughed. "Oh, it's nothing. I'm sure I get more out of it than they do."

Walking away, Jack suddenly turned back to the pro.

"It's the darndest thing, Ernie," he said, shaking his head. "I mean, how that slump just went away. One day it had taken me over, the next day it was gone. I don't know how or why it disappeared—only that it did. A real mystery, huh?"

The pro just shrugged. "Yeah, a real mystery," he replied, trying his best to suppress a grin.

THE RULES

A GENTLEMAN'S GAME

"Golf is in the interest of good health and good manners. It promotes self-interest and affords a chance to play the man and act the gentleman."

William Howard Taft

"Golf is the only game in the world in which a precise knowledge of the rules can earn one a reputation for bad sportsmanship."
Patrick Campbell, in Wit & Wisdom of Golf

"If you ask me, sir, it breaks to your right. And it's downhill, so don't swing too hard. Just give it a gentle nudge."

Warren Frazier, clad in a bright red pullover, a green sun visor and white knickers, peered over his half-moon glasses at his secretary some thirty feet away. "Nonsense, Miss Jones, it breaks to the left—and it's a perfectly level putt. I ought to know: Riverdale is my golf club; I play here every weekend. Besides, I didn't ask for your opinion. Now, just pull the pin please."

With that, the Senior Partner bent over the ball, lined up slightly to the right, glanced at the hole, waggled twice, then struck with a firm rap. The ball veered sharply to the right, rolling eight feet past the cup. From there, he two-putted for a double-bogey.

"Oh, what a beautiful day," chirped the matronly secretary, her white cotton blouse and silver hair flapping in the mild summer breeze as she steered the golf cart along the gravel path to the second tee. "A golf outing for the lawyers was a marvelous idea, Mr. Frazier. It should do wonders for morale."

Warren, at that moment more absorbed in the "6" Miss Jones had meticulously penciled in on the scorecard than in the weather or employee morale, looked up and smiled stiffly.

"Yes, yes indeed, Miss Jones. Morale has been sagging a bit of late. And now we have the summer clerks with us from the law schools. They're our future, you know. I want to impress them that we're not the stuffy, stodgy law firm we're sometimes reputed to be. We're sensitive people. At Frazier & Frazier, we practice law with a human face."

"Of course," Miss Jones replied. "But it's such a shame none of the summer lawyers could make it. I hear the two who were supposed to play with you are pretty fair golfers. In fact, someone told me that Jennifer Goodwin is a four handicap!"

The Senior Partner, his eyes averted, nervously cleared his throat. "Well, that happens. Something unexpected came up in the Amalgamated anti-trust case, and we needed the summer clerks to spend the day in the library doing important legal research."

"But the Amalgamated case isn't coming to trial for another year . . . ."

"Just drive, Miss Jones."

After Warren teed off on number two (slicing the ball up against the boundary fence to the right of the fairway), the skeptical secretary continued her pursuit.

"But I still don't understand why you're playing by yourself — and with me following you around! Every other lawyer is in a foursome. Couldn't you have been paired with someone else?"

"That wasn't necessary, Miss Jones. In fact, that's why I asked you to join me today. You're what is known in the golf world as my 'marker.' You're here to keep score — and to keep me honest. The pro OK'd it."

"A marker," the secretary repeated. "Sounds important!"

Miss Jones soon found out what the Senior Partner meant by "honest." Finding himself stymied, unable to swing, Warren lifted his ball, brushed a speck of mud from its surface and placed it carefully on a tuft of grass five feet from the fence. He proceeded to knock it onto the green with a three iron. From there, he got down in two.

"Give me a four, Miss Jones," Warren said, a self-satisfied smile on his face. "A well-deserved par."

The secretary, her eyebrows arched, stared at the Senior Partner. "But I counted five strokes, including the one stroke penalty for taking relief at the fence back there."

Warren glared at his scorekeeper. "Ridiculous! That fence is an artificial obstruction. I get a free drop."

"I beg to differ," Miss Jones persisted, removing a small white booklet from the back pocket of her green and white checkered slacks.

"What is that, Miss Jones?"

"The Rules of Golf, sir. Since I've never played the game, I wanted to make sure I understood the rules. I spent all last evening poring through this book, even highlighting the most important ones in magic marker. My goodness! They're more complicated than the Internal Revenue Code."

The secretary quickly thumbed through several pages. "Oh, here it is—Rule 24. It says an artificial obstruction does not include—and I quote—'objects defining out of bounds, such as walls, fences,' et cetera. See, I marked it . . . ."

"Forget it. At Riverdale, the members take a free drop from that fence. It's a local rule. Just put down a four and let's get on to the next tee."

Further misunderstandings were avoided until the sixth hole, a short par three, where Warren flew his tee shot into an enormous bunker behind the green. After a mighty explosion shot, accompanied by a thick cloud of sand, stone and dust, his ball came to rest but two feet from its original location, still in the trap. No sooner had the debris settled than the normally dignified attorney began pounding his club into the sand as if a venomous snake had just slithered into the bunker, a string of expletives spewing forth from his mouth like rapid fire from an assault rifle. Once he calmed down, Warren knocked his next shot ten feet from the pin, then sank the putt.

"A four," he brayed.

The secretary once more pulled out her rule book. "But, Mr. Frazier, Rule 13-4 clearly states that you cannot ground your club in a bunker without incurring a two-stroke penalty. I saw you hammer your wedge into the trap at least six times, so you really ought to be taking a sixteen, shouldn't you?"

Warren, maintaining his composure, smiled condescendingly.

"Very astute of you, Miss Jones. But you will note that the Rule also states that a player may touch the ground in a hazard to—if I remember the words correctly—'smooth sand or soil,' so long as he doesn't improve his lie."

Miss Jones pursed her lips. "And you consider thrashing about in the bunker in a maniacal frenzy to be smoothing the sand? Only a lawyer . . . ."

"Miss Jones, mark down a four."

On the eighth, Warren stroked a sixty-foot putt to within three feet of the pin.

"Good putt!" the secretary chimed. "Now, take your time with the next one. It looks like it has a tricky break."

Warren approached the hole, casting furtive glances in all directions as he neared the cup. When he reached his ball, he bent down, picked it up and put it in his pocket. "Give me a par."

"But you didn't hole out . . . ."

The Senior Partner took his secretary by the arm and led her, like a small child, to the edge of the green.

"Miss Jones," he said, removing his visor and running his fingers through his thinning gray hair, "let me explain a few things to you. First of all, you should understand that golf is a gentleman's game."

"A gentleman's game, sir?"

"Absolutely. The sport is quite different from the practice of law. Out here on the links, unlike in a courtroom, we don't focus on technicalities—like, say, holing out short putts. Only professionals are sticklers for the rules of golf—just like we lawyers are sticklers for the rules of the law. That three-footer was, by the standards of even the most rigorous amateur practitioner of this dismal science, a 'gimme.'"

Warren eyed his secretary to gauge her reaction. All he received in return was an incredulous stare.

"Second," he continued, "remember that you have been my secretary for twenty years. We're a team. And, as my teammate, I expect—indeed, I insist on—your full understanding, cooperation and support in whatever I do.

"Now, stop acting like my mother and start acting like my subordinate . . . I mean, my secretary. Put away that damn rule book and be supportive!"

Miss Jones seemed to have no choice but to comply. For the balance of the round, she endured, in stony silence, Warren Frazier's peculiar brand of golf. She said nothing when he, among other things, hit a "mulligan" for his tee shot at the eleventh hole; declared a small creek criss-crossing the twelfth fairway to be "casual water"; took a free drop for a ball "embedded" in a cavernous ditch behind the thirteenth green; and "gave" himself putts of four feet, five feet and seven feet, respectively, on the fourteenth, sixteenth and seventeenth holes.

"A four, Miss Jones," Warren called out as his secretary replaced the flag on the final hole. "That gives me an eighty-one for the round. With an eighteen handicap, that's a net sixty-three. Should put me right there in the hunt."

"Whatever you say," she said with a thinly-disguised smirk. "I'll hand in the scorecard."

Back at the cart shed, the deliriously happy Warren was oblivious to his secretary as she scampered away toward the pro shop.

For the next hour, a legion of disgruntled lawyers came in off the course, many shaking their heads in disgust. Warren beamed as, self-congratulatory scotch and soda already in hand, he listened to their complaints.

"I don't believe those greens; I couldn't make a putt over two feet to save my life!"

"That's nothing. I had an unplayable lie against that fence on the second hole, and then I hit two balls out on eleven!"

"If you want a horror story, that creek on twelve swallowed up three of my balls; I took a ten!"

"What about me? My playing partner charged me a one stroke penalty when the wind moved my ball on six, and then, on my bunker shot on fourteen, he charged me another two strokes when my wedge grazed the sand on my back swing."

Finally, Ernie Evans, the lanky, white-haired pro, emerged from the clubhouse, carrying a stack of scorecards. He began to post the final numbers on the board: Brickhouse—101 Gross, 82 Net; Thomas—87 Gross, 72 Net; Sullivan–120 Gross,

93 Net . . . . When he had recorded every score but Warren's, the pro scrutinized the remaining card and shook his head. "DQ" he marked, in black, opposite the Senior Partner's name.

Immediately, there could be heard a cry of "What!", together with the sound of a glass shattering on the patio tile.

"Disqualified!" Warren sputtered, as several firm associates ran over to render assistance to the tottering leader of the firm. "What do you mean, disqualified?"

Evans shrugged. "I'm sorry, Warren, but you didn't sign your scorecard. In fact, it looks like you didn't even read it. That disqualifies you."

He thrust the card at Warren, who gazed at the signature block in horror.

SCORER: PLAYER:

[s] Doris Jones [s] Warren Frazier by Doris Jones

(His Secretary)

DICTATED BUT NOT READ

Warren argued vehemently, but to no avail. "The rules require that each competitor verify and sign the scorecard. Miss Jones was your marker, and she couldn't sign for you. But you play here all the time, Warren. You know we insist on strict compliance with the rules."

"Miss Jones!" Warren bellowed like a wounded animal.

In a moment, the secretary, a margarita in hand, emerged from the clubhouse. "Yes, Mr. Frazier?" she asked in seeming innocence.

Warren, trying to contain his anger in front of the other lawyers, explained the problem.

"Oh, I'm sorry, sir," she said, taking a delicate sip from her drink. "I thought we were a team. And you said I should start acting like a secretary, so I did: I signed the card for you—like I sign your correspondence. I would have double-checked the rule with you, but you told me to put the rule book away. Well, at least you had an enjoyable time out there today, with the sunshine, the fresh air, the exercise, the camaraderie, the . . . ."

"Can it, Miss Jones," Warren growled, as he turned and stomped away toward the cart shed.

Retrieving his personal belongings from the cart, Warren noticed that Miss Jones had left her copy of the Rules of Golf on the seat. It was opened to the section entitled "Player's Responsibilities." Warren read a passage highlighted in pink magic marker:

> *After completion of the round, the competitor should check his score for each hole . . . ensure that the marker has signed the card, countersign the card himself and return it.*

He grimaced, then tore the booklet to shreds.

"A gentleman's game," he muttered through clenched teeth as he hurled the shreds into the air and gave a good, swift kick to his bag.

THE LORE

THE LUCKY SHOES

"In every other part of my life, I am the embodiment of the rational, logical, no-nonsense man. I don't read horoscopes, never feel destined to win the lottery and never make a detour around an ominous ladder. But when it comes to golf, I (and many of my golfing friends) are like tremulous primitives, seething with superstitions and shamanistic rituals."

Lee Bacchus Looks at Golf

"It's not fair, Ernie—it's just not fair!" complained Leland Porter, glaring at Ernie Evans across the pro shop display case. "You have no right to tell members what kind of shoes to wear. It's downright . . . un-American!"

The lanky, white-haired Evans chuckled. "What do you mean, Leland? We've always had dress standards around here—shirts with collars, knee-length Bermudas, no halter-tops."

"But shoes are different. Every American's got the right to wear the footwear of his or her choice—Nikes, Addidas, Reeboks . . . ."

The skeptical pro shook his head. "Give me a break," he said. "You just want to keep wearing those godawful 'lucky' shoes of yours. You're superstitious—admit it!"

Porter turned red. "This isn't about me," he said defensively. "It's a question of principle!"

With that, the disgruntled member stormed out the door in a huff.

•   •   •   •   •

When the veteran pro had banned metal spikes from the course, effective July 4, he hadn't been thinking about Leland Porter. He'd been thinking about the havoc to the greens wrought by traditional cleats, and about how most courses now required players to wear "soft" spikes made of rubber or plastic. He hadn't considered the impact of his decision on the five-term Mayor of River Grove and his "Lucky Shoes."

Although superstitions abounded at the Riverdale Golf and Country Club, none was embraced as fervently as Porter's belief in the mystical powers of his golf shoes. The stout, gray-haired politico insisted on wearing the same pair of black leather Wilson "Everlasts" — purchased fifteen years before at brother-in-law Mike Dagostino's Downtown Discount Sports Super Store — he'd worn the day he'd taken the Third Flight of the Men's Golf Championship from the late Tom Dunphy. In Porter's mind, the decrepit shoes — scuffed, nicked and worn to the point that they resembled the footwear in vogue at Valley Forge in 1777 — were as necessary to playing golf as woods and irons. He hadn't replaced so much as a shoelace since he'd first donned them.

"STAND UP FOR PERSONAL FREEDOM!" read the computer-generated handbill taped to every locker the next morning. "AFFIRM MEMBER RIGHTS! JOIN IN PETITIONING THE RIVERDALE BOARD TO RESCIND THE BAN ON METAL SPIKES! — Leland H. Porter."

The pro was soon inundated with complaints.

"Say, Ernie, what's this about us having to buy new golf shoes?" asked senior member Tom Sargeant one afternoon as Evans restocked his supply of soft-spiked FootJoys. "What with dues, cart fees and food minimums, not to mention the cost of shirts, hats, gloves, balls and sun screen, we're already paying through the nose around here. Some of us are on fixed incomes, you know!"

Evans grimaced. "Who told you you'd have to buy new shoes, Tom?"

"Why, Mayor Porter. He didn't say it in so many words, but I got the message."

Evans explained that new shoes were optional and that replacement cleats would suffice.

Sargeant nevertheless persisted. "Even so, I bet you'll charge us an arm and a leg for the new spikes — and for refitting the shoes."

Next approached by Lester Norman, a middle-aged member suffering the effects of an old football injury, Evans found himself dabbling in both physics and orthopedics.

"Are soft spikes really safe, Ernie? Will they cling to the turf when you swing? I'd hate to aggravate my knee coming down hard on the ball."

Evans opined that there was no difference in traction between the hard and soft spikes, except, perhaps, on steep grades.

"You mean, like the hill bordering fifteen?" Norman retorted. "I'm up there all the time. Do I have to risk breaking my neck just to play it? Leland warned me about your radical ideas!"

Later that day, Evans was accosted in the clubhouse snack bar by two ruffled lady members.

"Shame on you, Ernie," one (an overweight matron in her fifties) scolded, wagging a chubby finger in his face. "I've heard about your plan to ban golf carts. With my heart condition, I couldn't survive if I had to walk the course!"

"And what about eliminating the ladies tees?" the other (a frail woman in her sixties) interjected. "Without them, I could never hit over the canyon on seven, the bunker on nine or the water on eighteen!"

The pro shook his head and sighed. "Ladies, I'm proposing nothing of the sort. Who told you I was—Leland Porter, by any chance?"

The women nodded in unison. "Of course," confessed one, "he didn't actually say you were going to do those things, but he suggested you *might* if we let you to get away with requiring soft spikes."

Weary of Porter's misrepresentations, Evans asked member (and fellow sporting goods merchant) Mike Dagostino to "talk some sense into your thick-headed brother-in-law."

Dagostino, normally an enthusiastic proponent of any new piece of equipment or accessory that would bring in business at his downtown store, hesitated. "Uh . . . er . . . I think I'll stay out of this one, Ernie," he said sheepishly. "I've sort of got a conflict of interest."

Frustrated, the pro finally confronted the ex-Mayor in the men's locker room.

"Leland, stop acting like a politician and tell the truth for once! This isn't an election, you know. Just fess up to your superstition about those damn shoes."

"Ernie, you wound me deeply," the politician countered, an expression of shock and pain on his face. "Integrity is my middle name. This campaign—I mean, my petition to the Board—isn't about me. It's a matter of principle!"

"But you're getting everyone all riled up."

"Good! They should be!"

• • • • •

Porter's influence on his fellow Riverdalers was all too evident on the Fourth of July when nearly half those scheduled to compete in the Independence Day Scramble arrived in metal cleats, many defiantly sporting buttons displaying a FootJoy golf shoe with a red "X" superimposed upon it.

"We won't be moved," Porter announced to the pro. "Either we play in shoes of our own choosing, or there won't be a tournament."

Quickly intervening, Ross Griswald, the Club's portly Chairman, immediately declared a two-week moratorium on the metal spike ban, pending reconsideration of the matter by the Board.

For days afterward, Ernie Evans brooded. To his mind, the former Mayor was as ethically challenged as a golfer who kicks his ball out of a bunker or pencils in a par after taking bogey. Convinced of the righteousness of his cause, Evans decided to fight back, composing, with Ross Griswald's approval, an "Open Letter to Riverdalers." Posted on all clubhouse bulletin boards and stuffed into every locker, the letter accused Porter of promoting "voodoo golf."

> Like the politician that he is, the Honorable Mr. Porter has declined to reveal his true motive in opposing soft spikes. Posing as the champion of personal freedom and a defender of the elderly, the physically-challenged and women, the Mayor has cynically masked his real objective: to continue wearing an unsightly pair of worn-out, steel-spiked golf shoes he considers "lucky."

Evans was confident that members would listen to reason.

• • • • •

The second-floor meeting room was packed by the time the Board took up the matter of soft spikes and Evans rose to address the issue.

"Very persuasive, Ernie," intoned Ross Griswald after the pro had made his case for the new policy. "Now, Leland, do you have anything to say in rebuttal?"

Shaking his head sadly, the ex-Mayor stood up and approached the podium. Dressed in a gray, double-breasted suit, a "No Soft Spikes" button pinned to one lapel and a miniature American flag to the other, he began by tearing in two what he described as "my prepared remarks" in order, he said, "to speak from my heart."

As Evans fought to restrain a derisive groan, the speaker expressed dismay that the pro had "taken the low road, reducing this debate to the level of a personal vendetta against a member."

Porter had to raise his hand to silence cries of "Shame! Shame!" erupting from the audience.

"My opponent — I mean, our Club professional — has sought to belittle my position by attacking my integrity. He accuses me of secretly harboring a 'silly personal superstition.'"

As beads of perspiration formed on his brow, Porter requested a glass of water. Taking a small sip, he cleared his throat and continued.

"My friends, do we all not have our own personal habits, routines, rituals, preferences and quirks? Some stay home on Friday the Thirteenth, others avoid walking beneath ladders and still others jump at the sight of a black cat. In golf, some take practice swings before striking the ball; others wiggle their hips; still others flex their knees. Who is to say such habits are wrong — are 'silly?' Who is to say we have no right to have them? Is not one man's (or woman's) superstition another's reality?"

The former Mayor paused. Then, with an almost demonic grin on his face, he left the podium and approached the Board.

"Myrtle," he asked perennial Women's Golf Champion, Myrtle Anderson, "don't you always wear something green when you play?"

The tall, angular champion squirmed uneasily in her seat. "Well . . . yes . . . I suppose I do," she sputtered. "But it was the color I was wearing when I first met my husband!"

A titter of laughter arose from the audience. Porter turned to Ross Griswald. "And you, Ross—why is that you always toss a penny into the water hazard on ten? Could it be you're seeking favor from the golf gods?"

"Uh . . . er . . . it can't hurt," was all the Chairman could muster in his defense.

But the politician had saved his best for last. Turning to Ernie Evans, he pointed an accusing finger at the pro. "And you, Ernie. Why do you always mark your ball with three red dots? Do you think it's lucky?"

The pro's jaw dropped. The politician had somehow discovered his practice—the reason for which he had long since forgotten—of always using a trio of red dots to identify his ball. He'd never considered it a superstition—just, well, sort of a habit . . . a routine . . . a ritual . . . a preference . . . a quirk.

Although protesting ("my dots don't damage the greens, Leland"), the pro admitted to the charge. With that, his support among the Board vanished like an errant tee shot into a lateral hazard. After a brief recess, the directors announced their decision to "grandfather" from metal spike ban any shoe owned by a Club member on the effective date of the new policy, set as the following Labor Day.

•   •   •   •   •

As the summer progressed, Ernie Evans found himself unable to move his inventory of soft spikes and soft-spiked shoes.

"Sorry I caused you so much trouble, Ernie," said Leland Porter as he stood in the pro shop that Labor Day, peering at a sign announcing "NEW FOOTJOYS WITH SOFT SPIKES—ORIGINALLY $129.99 A PAIR—NOW ONLY $79.98." "I hope you're not angry with me."

The pro shook his head. "Angry?" he replied. "No, I'm not angry. In fact, I consider myself the victor in our little dispute. I actually got you to admit the truth. That's pretty rare for a politician."

"Uh . . . if you say so."

"But your brother-in-law must be livid," Evans continued. "I'm sure he's swimming in soft spikes down at his store."

Porter lifted a box of FootJoys off the table, removed a shoe and examined its rubber cleats. "Actually, Ernie," he replied, "Mike's doing just fine. You see, he took a flyer on metal-spiked golf shoes this spring, so the Board's decision turned out to be a God-send. After the meeting, he unloaded all his inventory at premium prices. He even repaid all the money he owed me. Guess you could say we both got lucky, huh?"

The pro stared blankly as Porter tried on the shoe. "By the way, Ernie, my old shoes can't last forever. Plus, they never did fit very well. And I suppose that superstition of mine is a bit . . . silly. Anyway, when these FootJoys come down to $59.95, could you give me a call? Maybe we can do business."

The pro stared steely-eyed at his foe, his jaw muscles tense. "Of course, Leland," he said. "I'll make sure you're the first to know!"

SENIORS

GOING FOR THE GOLD

"Golf holds out hope of improvement longer than any other sport, but does there not come a time when even the most avid collector of tips and lessons must face the fact that his handicap will never be lower than it is? When a perfectly nailed drive, whizzing forward like a rocket, somehow winds up thirty yards short of the drives of yesteryear? When even the head of the putter seems heavy? When not a thousand dollars worth of new metal woods engineered by half the geniuses in Texas will stem the inexorable erosion of developed skills? Then the game asks our love not as the repository of infinite possibilities that it once was but as a measure of our finitude. Everything has dwindled but, perhaps, our bliss."

John Updike, Golf Dreams

"Let's see you top that, old timer!" Jonathan Herron gloated, scooping up his broken tee as his ball came to rest some two hundred fifty yards down the fairway.

"I don't have to," replied Sidney Owen, ambling to the front tee box, leaning on his driver like a cane. "At my age, I've got nothing left to prove. All that's important is getting around in fewer strokes than you."

Herron, a swarthy young man with the physique and demeanor of a professional wrestler, grunted as his slight, white-haired opponent, dressed in baggy Bermuda shorts, a faded green golf shirt and a soiled yellow visor, approached the gold markers, bent over stiffly and placed his ball on a plastic tee. Swinging easily, Sidney knocked it into the right center of the fairway, sixty yards short of Herron.

"Not too shabby for a seventy-three year-old with arthritis," Sidney gently taunted his opponent as the two drove away along the bumpy cart path. "But, then, golf is primarily a mental game, don't you agree?"

"Yeah, sure," Herron sneered. "And you've got me psyched out already. I mean, how am I supposed to compete with you teeing off twenty to fifty yards in front of me on every hole? It's not fair!"

"Quit grousing, Jonathan," Sidney chided the younger man, widely considered not only a sandbagger, but a poor sport to boot, among the members of the Riverdale Golf and Country Club. "Rules are rules: Ernie said you play from the white tees, I play from the gold. Besides, it's all reflected in our handicaps, so we're competing on a level playing field."

But the yardage difference grated on Sidney. Deep down, he felt it gave him an unfair advantage — if only psychological. He wished they'd never put in those damn gold tee markers. "Viagra Tees," the younger players called them. And, to make matters worse, the Club required everyone over seventy to play from them. "We don't want the senior players holding everybody up, trying to prove they can still hit like Tiger Woods," pro Ernie Evans had said. In Sidney's mind, it was like playing with souped-up balls and super-charged clubs.

Standing beside his ball, Sidney remembered the day, years before, when he'd beaten Gil James to win this event. A two-handicapper then, competing in the championship flight and playing from the back tees, he'd rifled his drive past the one-fifty marker, then knocked it stiff with an eight iron. Now, relegated to the "Gentleman's Flight" (reserved for members with "loftier" handicaps), Sidney found himself over two hundred yards from the flag. He took out a three wood and stroked the ball forty yards short of the green. From there, he got down in three, beating Herron, who'd put his second shot into the water to the left, by a stroke.

Throughout the overcast afternoon, the two men engaged in a seesaw battle, Herron playing the young man's game of daring and power, Sidney the old man's game of caution and finesse. On the par five third, Herron took a one-stroke lead when, challenging the creek that criss-crossed the fairway from tee to green, he reached in two and birdied, while the plodding Sidney, laying up, lipped the cup on his par attempt. On the seventh, Sidney regained the lead when Herron topped his drive into the gully off the tee, while Sidney, teeing-up on the far side, hit the green in regulation and made four. Sidney increased his lead on nine when Herron's five-iron shot landed in the right-side bunker, while Sidney's shorter seven wood dribbled on and he two-putted.

"Doesn't your conscience bother you, Sidney?" Herron complained in the snack bar at the turn. "I have to hit over creeks, canyons and God knows what else, while you've got nothing but wide-open fairway to shoot at. I mean, first Social Security, then Medicare—and now gold tee markers. I can't wait to get old!"

Sidney, his face flushed, tried to appear nonchalant. "I don't feel a bit guilty, Jonathan," he lied, popping an Advil tablet as if to emphasize his frailty. "Your problems are all in your head."

On the back side, Herron briefly regained the lead on the fifteenth, only to give back two strokes on sixteen when he dumped his drive into a clump of bushes by the ladies' tee box, where Sidney once again hit from the gold markers. Herron then pulled to within one stroke by parring seventeen while Sidney bogeyed.

"I might as well throw in the towel," Herron complained as he emerged from the cart alongside the eighteenth tee. Before them stretched a familiar expanse of water, a small peninsula jutting out near the far side, bordered by menacing-looking rocks. "It's at least a one-seventy-five carry from here," Herron barked, brandishing his oversized driver in Sidney's face like the butt of a rifle. "For you, from the peninsula—or should I say, from the ladies' tee—it couldn't be more than sixty!"

Sidney, his adrenalin pumping from his sudden one-stroke advantage, slammed his driver on the ground. "Goddamn it, Jonathan, I've had it with your excuses. Tell you what. Just to shut you up, I'll tee off from the whites. And, to make it interesting, I'll bet you five bucks I clear the water!"

Herron, gazing across the hazard, grinned like a toddler presented a dish of chocolate ice cream. "You're on, old fossil."

Herron smashed a towering drive that cleared the lake by fifty yards on the fly. As his opponent yielded the tee, Sidney's heart was pounding and his throat was dry. He hadn't hit from this tee box in years.

Sidney bent over, pulled up a tuft of grass and tossed it into the air. He smiled as the blades drifted lazily toward the water. He placed his ball on the tee, took two practice swings, looked down the fairway, flexed his spindly legs, waggled twice and then swung with all his might.

He hit a high, arcing shot. As the ball rose in the air, it looked certain to cross the hazard. But then, as it descended, the outcome seemed in doubt. Sidney froze. "Please, just this once," he whispered in the wind. When the ball reached ground level, it suddenly disappeared. Expecting a splash, Sidney instead heard a sharp "clack," then watched as the ball bounded off the rocks, flew forward and came to rest ten yards ahead of Herron.

The younger man stood and stared in silence. "Thank you, thank you," Sidney muttered, kissing the shaft of his club.

It was sweet—a tee shot for the Ages.

•　　　•　　　•　　　•　　　•

Each man holed out for par.

"Good match," Jonathan Herron said with a stiff smile, shaking Sidney's outstretched hand and planting a five-dollar bill in it as they left the green. "That was some drive. I'll bet you never hit another like it as long as you live."

"Probably not," Sidney sighed. "That's why I had to try."

Herron's smile quickly vanished. "Unfortunately, I'm going to have you disqualified for hitting from the wrong tees back there. It's the rule, you know."

Herron reached into his bag and retrieved an immaculate copy of the Rules of Golf. "Now, it may not seem fair . . . ."

Sidney waved him off. "Don't bother, Jonathan: fair or not, I know you've got me. I guess I let my ego get the best of me. Pretty stupid, huh?"

Herron slapped the older man on the back. "Well, at least you're being a good sport about it. To tell you the truth, I'd been trying to goad you into that all day. But what I don't understand is how a smart guy like you could have fallen for it. It couldn't have been for a measly five bucks. It's almost as if you . . . you threw the match!"

Sidney simply shrugged. "I must be getting senile."

The victorious Herron nodded smugly. "But, then again, maybe I know something you don't," Sidney added with a playful chuckle, tossing his ball over his shoulder to an imaginary crowd of cheering spectators lining the fairway and the green.

JUNIORS

THE KID

"Golf, like measles, should be caught young."
   P.G. Wodehouse, in Freeman, *The Golfer's Book of Wisdom*

"But of all things, let not the young player get irritated by the luck of the green being apparently against him. Let him bravely defy his luck, and if he be a philosopher, even thank the fall that has given him some useful experience."
   H.B. Fannie, in *Wit & Wisdom of Golf*

When Ernie Evans declared Charlie Kim eligible to compete in the Club Championship tournament, it touched off a storm of protest at the Riverdale Golf and Country Club. It was the pro's most controversial decision since disqualifying Tim Tucker from the Labor Day Classic for arriving ten minutes late on the first tee.

"Are you crazy, Ernie?" complained one disgruntled member after Evans had placed Charlie's name on the list of the sixteen qualifiers for the First Flight. "I thought this was the *Men's* Club Championship. What next—are the ladies going to compete?"

"Absolutely ridiculous," another member protested to the lanky, white-haired pro. "How can you let Charlie Kim play? He's not even allowed in the Men's Locker Room Bar!"

"Surely, there's been some mistake," other bewildered members said. "Charlie Kim's only a kid!"

Charles Franklin Kim was, in fact, fifteen years old. Even worse, the short, cherubic Charlie looked about ten—and played golf like a seasoned veteran.

Charlie and his father, Sung Lee Kim, were no strangers to controversy. Years before, when the Korean-born Sung—an executive at a local electronics firm—was denied membership at Riverdale, he brought a lawsuit claiming the Club systematically discriminated against minorities. To settle the suit, the Board created a special class of membership for non-citizens. "International Members" (as they were styled) were required to renew their memberships every five years and, unlike "Regular Members," had no ownership interest in the Club.

Later, after complaints that International Members (almost all Asian nationals) were holding up play, the Board ruled that only Regular Members could tee off before ten on weekends. No sooner had they acted than the Kims appeared at the pro shop early one Saturday morning demanding a starting time.

"But Mr. Kim," Ernie Evans pleaded. "You and Charlie have always played in the afternoons. Why change now?"

The thin, bespectacled Sung Lee Kim smiled stiffly. "I'm sorry, Mr. Evans," he replied politely, "but this is a matter of principle. We are proud people, and only ask to be treated fairly."

"But I'm a golf professional, not a social worker . . . ."

"You are, however, in charge of regulating play."

"Okay, okay," Evans said, raising his hands in mock surrender. "I'll see what I can do!"

Despite grumbling by those huddled around the cart shed waiting to go off, Evans, after waking up Ross Griswald, the Chairman of the Board, for his concurrence, let the two tee off at eight-ten. He could convince no one, however, to play with them.

"Thank you, Mr. Evans," Charlie said afterward. "We're not trying to make trouble. But we have to defend our rights. If we don't, people will walk all over us."

"I just don't want to mess with those two," Evans confessed when asked to explain his decision to let Charlie compete. "Besides," he added, waving a dog-eared copy of the Club's By-Laws in the air, "the rules say 'all male Members in good standing shall be eligible.' All you have to be is 'male'; you don't have to be a 'man.' Anyway, pound-for-pound, Charlie Kim may be the best golfer we have around here."

Few would disagree with this assessment. Having taken up the game at the age of eight, Charlie had, with his father's encouragement, diligent practice and regular lessons, succeeded in becoming a golfing prodigy. The reigning Junior

Champion, Charlie was not only capable of conquering the challenging Riverdale eighteen, but possessed an uncanny ability to rattle opponents. Perhaps it was the sight of the boyish-looking teenager driving the ball 250 yards down the center of the fairway, or, barely visible in a deep bunker, blasting to within a foot of the pin, or, squinting through thick, rimless glasses, knocking a sixty-foot putt into the center of the cup; or perhaps it was his inscrutable demeanor: whatever it was, many talented players faltered when taking on Charlie Kim.

•　　　•　　　•　　　•　　　•

Charlie easily dispatched his first two opponents. He beat Sandy Jenkins, five and four, by holing a chip shot from the edge of the fourteenth green for a birdie. Pete Arnold conceded his match to Charlie after knocking two balls out of bounds off the fifteenth tee.

"There was no point in continuing," Arnold told Evans. "The kid had me spooked. There's something *different* about him . . . ."

"Stop griping, Pete," the pro replied. "Charlie's just a normal teenager. The only thing different about him is that he can beat the pants off you older guys."

"Well, the little runt doesn't bother me," barked Hank Girard, striding into the pro shop after defeating Tom Irving to become Charlie's semi-final opponent. "He may have raw talent, but he lacks finesse. A boy can't play a man's game."

The following Saturday, while Evans reviewed the rules with the players on the first tee, the six-foot-two Girard stood toe-to-toe with his four-foot-ten adversary, staring him down like a heavyweight at center ring. "May the better man win," boomed Girard, giving Charlie a bone-crushing handshake. Charlie just nodded, saying nothing.

When the two made the turn, Girard was beaming. "I'm three holes up," he boasted to the pro. "I'm trouncing this kid!"

Charlie sat passively in the cart, betraying no emotion.

Two hours later, the pair returned to the cart shed. Girard looked stunned, as if he had just taken a sucker punch from his diminutive opponent.

"The kid beat me," he groaned, handing Evans the scorecard.

"He had too many clubs in his bag, Mr. Evans," Charlie said matter-of-factly.

Evans counted Girard's clubs. There were fifteen—one over the limit.

"I guess I put my four wood in without taking out my two iron," Girard said dejectedly. "But I didn't use either one. And the kid didn't tell me until I holed out on eighteen. I was winning . . . ."

"It makes no difference," Charlie countered. "Players are limited to fourteen clubs, whether they use them all or not. And it wasn't my fault you violated the rule!"

"I'm afraid he's right," Evans agreed with a sigh.

Later, the pro confronted the young winner in the clubhouse. "Charlie, I think you knew all along that Hank was carrying too many clubs. But you let him play anyway, waiting until it was to your advantage to tell him. You call that fair?"

The youngster stared at Evans impassively. "Mr. Evans," he replied coolly, "I'm not the one who violated the rules. Anyway, he would have done the same thing to me—any member here would have."

The pro gritted his teeth. "I'm glad you're so sure of yourself."

Charlie just turned and walked away.

•   •   •   •   •

The outcome of the Girard-Kim match created a furor at the normally tranquil country club.

"Somebody ought to teach that kid a lesson," one irate member said. "Obviously, his father never taught him good sportsmanship. Maybe we should educate him."

"Why bother?" another said. "I mean, they're all alike! They don't try to get along. They're clannish, keep to themselves, never mix in or try to be friendly. They don't belong here."

Evans had given up defending Charlie. "I guess I misjudged him," he said, shaking his head. "He hasn't grown up yet . . . ."

The title match, pitting Charlie against Bill Davis, the defending champion, was held the following Saturday.

As in prior Championships, Evans closed the course to permit members to watch the action. Usually, a horde of golf enthusiasts showed up. On this day, however, only a handful of spectators appeared. The few who did attend were there to support Bill Davis.

"I guess the threat of rain kept people away," Evans said, pointing to the overcast sky.

"Yeah, sure," Charlie said, looking around the largely deserted tee area. "Let's just get on with it, okay?"

The pro officiated the contest.

Neither player was at his best that morning. Charlie failed to capitalize on Davis's poor iron play, missing short putts to win on three holes. On the eighth, after Charlie knocked his drive out of bounds, Davis—considered the best sand player at the Club—barely managed to tie, taking three shots to get out of a bunker. Both double-bogeyed the ninth.

In spite of Davis's weak performance, the small cadre of spectators cheered whenever he hit a shot; Charlie's play was greeted with polite but stony silence.

As the players stood on the tenth tee, the match even, Charlie gazed forlornly at the empty clubhouse grounds, looking like a little boy lost in a giant shopping mall.

"By the way, where's your Dad, Charlie?" Evans asked. "I thought he'd be here cheering you on. He's always come out for your Junior Championship matches."

The youngster frowned. "When I told him about my match with Mr. Girard, he said . . . uh . . . er . . . he said I was on my own."

Play improved on the back nine. Davis took the lead with birdies on ten and eleven; Charlie evened the match with birdies on twelve and thirteen. The two remained tied through seventeen.

On eighteen, both hit towering drives over the water into the center of the fairway. Davis sliced his second shot into a bunker. Charlie hit a high, arcing seven iron that flew the putting surface and bounded into the leafy ice plant behind the green.

Charlie's ball was nowhere to be seen. He waded into the thick vegetation and began rummaging around. When it became obvious that he was having no luck, Davis, Evans and the three remaining spectators joined in the hunt. Other members, watching from the clubhouse balcony, came down to assist.

Soon, a small volunteer army was engaged in the search. For five minutes, they combed the area like concerned neighbors looking for a child who has wandered off. Whenever a ball was sighted, Charlie would run over to examine it, only to discover that it wasn't his.

"Thanks everyone," he finally said. "It looks like it's gone." But just as he started walking back to replay his shot, Bill Davis called out to him. "There's a Pinnacle 1 back here, kid. Isn't that what you were playing?"

The ball was propped up on two rubbery leaves as if beckoning to be hit. Charlie couldn't have had a better lie if he had placed it there himself.

"Thank you," Charlie said, smiling for the first time that day. "You really didn't have to . . . ."

"You're right, I didn't," Davis replied curtly. "But maybe you can return the favor some day."

A red-faced Charlie knocked his next shot three feet from the cup. Davis's sand shot came up ten feet short, and he two-putted for a bogey. Charlie tapped in to win.

•　　•　　•　　•　　•

Back in the pro shop, Ernie Evans was sitting at the computer, knocking out an announcement of Charlie's victory, when the young man walked in, shaking his head and grinning.

"You're not going to believe this, Mr. Evans," he said, "but there's a problem."

The pro turned to Charlie and groaned audibly. He'd had enough of Charlie Kim's problems for one season. "Now what?"

Charlie placed a grass-stained golf ball in Evans's hand. "That's the ball I hit out of the ice plant on eighteen," he explained. "A Pinnacle 1."

"So?"

"It's not mine. I always mark my balls with two blue dots for identification. That one doesn't have any markings."

Evans examined the ball like an appraiser inspecting a fine diamond. "Well, maybe you forgot . . . ."

"That's impossible. That simply isn't mine. You have to disqualify me for playing the wrong ball, Mr. Evans. You have no choice."

Evans shook his head in frustration. "Dammit, Charlie! After everything I did to get you into this tournament, after all the excuses I made for you, now you're insisting I disqualify you? You sound as if you want to lose—as if you're proud . . . ."

"I appreciate everything you've done for me, Mr. Evans," Charlie said. "But, as my father said, we are proud people, and we treat others as fairly as we ask them to treat us. And that's why I want you to declare Mr. Davis the winner. It's only right."

•　　•　　•　　•　　•

Later that afternoon, Ernie Evans could be seen scouring the ice plant behind the eighteenth green. He was carrying a bucket filled with lost golf balls he'd retrieved from the leafy underbrush, none a Pinnacle 1 with two blue dots. "No, it couldn't be," the veteran pro was muttering to himself. "It couldn't be . . . ."

COUPLES

COUPLED

"Sudden success in golf is like the sudden acquisition of wealth. It is apt to unsettle and deteriorate the character."
  P.G. Wodehouse, in Freeman, The Golfer's Book of Wisdom

"Never insist that your spouse golf. It can lead to only two results. One, she/he plays really badly, complains for four hours and ruins your whole day. Or, he/she plays really well, offers four hours of suggestions on how you might do better and ruins your whole day."
  Ernie Whitham, in Chicken Soup for the Golfer's Soul

"Now there's a lucky guy," said Will Anderson, pointing out the pro shop window toward the tenth tee. "What I wouldn't give to be in his shoes!"

Ernie Evans, sitting behind the counter posting scores on his computer, donned his glasses and looked outside. "Oh, you mean Todd Lovett," he replied, spotting a wiry young man smashing a towering drive off the tee as a bronzed and beautiful blonde in Bermuda shorts looked on in admiration. "I guess he is lucky. Intelligent, good-looking, successful . . . ."

"And," Anderson sighed, "he can beat his wife at golf!"

The veteran pro chuckled. "Oh, come on, Will, it can't be all that bad—can it?"

"Ernie, if only—just once—I could show her up . . . ."

Just then, the door opened to reveal a tall, slender woman in a checkered blouse and green slacks, looking out through steel-rimmed spectacles from under a white safari hat.

"Oh, there you are," said Myrtle Anderson, clucking her tongue as if she had just stumbled upon a stray pet. "The Goldman's are waiting for us on the first tee. Get a move on or we'll forfeit the match!"

"Yes, dear," Will muttered, slinking toward the door like a convict ordered into lock-down. "Anything you say."

A prominent local attorney, Will Anderson was a firm believer in the equality of the sexes. He was proud of Myrtle's golfing talents, he told others. He could care less that she played to a three handicap, while he languished in double-digits; that she regularly drove the ball over two hundred yards, while he was often lucky to reach the fairway with a stiff wind at his back; or that she'd won every women's title at the Riverdale Golf and Country Club, while his best finish ever was a tie for third in the "Gentlemen's Flight" of the Men's Labor Day Classic.

But anyone who had ever seen the Andersons play couples golf—who had witnessed Will's silent exasperation when Myrtle drained a long putt, his dispirited demeanor when he flubbed an easy shot beneath her critical gaze, or his vacant expression when, back at the clubhouse, she would post a score ten to fifteen strokes lower than his—knew better. As golfing partners, the Andersons weren't so much a team as a standup routine, with Will cast in the role of bumbling sidekick.

"Back for more punishment, eh?" the rotund Gus Goldman, an unlit cigar dangling from his mouth, grunted as the Andersons joined their opponents on the first tee. "I would have thought that, after last year's drubbing, you two would have given up couples golf."

Will winced, remembering only too well how he and Myrtle had lost the prior year's Better Ball Championship to the Goldmans when, leading the final match at the turn, he began topping his shots and Myrtle, despite superhuman efforts, was unable to carry the team on the back nine.

"Now, dear, don't be a boor," chided the petite Evelyn Goldman. "We're here to have fun. Isn't that right, Myrtle?"

Myrtle glared at Gus Goldman with steely eyes. "We're gonna kick your butt, Gus!" she blurted out. "That is, if my partner here can get his act together!"

So much for fun, thought Will.

•   •   •   •   •

Expecting the worst, Will was unprepared for what was to transpire that day.

Thus, when his approach on the first hole rolled to within inches of the cup, giving the Andersons the early lead, the fatalistic Will chalked it up to blind luck. And when, after Myrtle dumped her drive out-of-bounds on number two, he knocked in a ninety-foot chip to tie the Goldmans, he told himself that it was pure coincidence.

But when, on three, he sank a forty-footer for a birdie, he knew something was up.

"Some putt," Gus Goldman grudgingly acknowledged as the foursome walked onto the next tee. "What's gotten into you, anyway?"

"I . . . I . . . don't know," Will stammered.

"Impressive," Myrtle Anderson added. "I've never seen you play like this before. It's a . . . a . . . miracle!"

Miracle or not, it was clear that Will Anderson was in "The Zone"—that mysterious realm in which a player, otherwise prone to bungle tee shots, botch approaches and foozle putts, is incapable of doing wrong—where errant drives bound off trees onto the fairway, poorly-hit irons carry hazards to land on the green, and putts that, on any other day, would miss the hole by a foot, drop into the cup—where bogies become pars, pars become birdies and the once-dreaded "others" become a distant memory—where, in short, he becomes invincible.

And so, while Myrtle hacked her way from tee to green, contributing nothing to the Anderson cause, Will put on a show of golfing prowess worthy of a touring professional. When scratch golfer Gus Goldman birdied the fifth, Will countered by blasting a sand shot to within four feet of the flag, sinking the putt and earning a high-five from a grateful Myrtle. And, on eight, when Evelyn Goldman put her two handicap strokes to good use by shooting a five, Will matched the feat by sinking a winding thirty-footer, eliciting a cry of "You Da Man!" from his normally staid mate. And, on nine, where both Goldmans netted pars, Will handily tied the hole with an up-and-down from the rough, leading the deliriously happy Myrtle to grab him around the waist, hoist him off the ground and kiss him like a returning war hero.

"I always knew you had it in you, darling," she cooed.

Driving their cart to the tenth tee, Will Anderson silently congratulated himself on having finally earned the respect of his wife on the golf course. He had, he told himself, achieved his most coveted objective.

•   •   •   •   •

Will's hot streak continued on the back side—a par on ten, a birdie on eleven, a par on twelve. Feeling incapable of doing wrong, he began ignoring Myrtle's advice, planting a three iron on the thirteenth green after she'd recommended a four wood, hitting a towering eight iron over a tree to the putting surface on fourteen after she'd counseled a safe lay up, and dropping a long putt on fifteen after she'd told him to "just lag it close."

"Listen, Myrtle," he complained as they headed to the sixteenth tee, "I'd appreciate it if you'd stop kibitzing. You're not being at all helpful."

"I'm sorry, darling," she replied contritely, "I'm doing the best I can."

"It's hard to tell," he snapped.

Unfortunately, despite Will's unprecedented performance, the Goldmans—through a combination of skill, bravado and just plain luck—took full advantage of Myrtle's poor play, staying within striking distance of their opponents. Only two down going into sixteen (where Myrtle hit her approach into the ice plant behind the green), they pulled to within one when Evelyn's sculled chip shot hit the flag on the fly and dropped into the hole, beating Will's sandy par from a buried lie in the left-hand bunker. On seventeen (where Myrtle hit two balls out-of-bounds off the tee), a birdie by Gus bested Will's solid four, evening the match.

"What's it like toting an extra bag around?" Gus taunted Will, thrusting a sharp elbow into his rib cage as they walked off the green, out of the hearing of their spouses. "Now you know how Myrtle's felt carrying you all these years!"

Suddenly, two decades of suppressed anger and resentment welled up inside Will, spilling over like refuse from a backed-up storm drain.

"Jesus, Myrtle!" he bellowed as they drove to the eighteenth tee. "Do you expect me to win all by myself? We're a team, after all!"

"Oh, darling, I'm so sorry . . . ."

"Sorry doesn't cut it . . . ."

Myrtle's eyes suddenly lit up and her face brightened. "Oh look, Will," she exclaimed, jumping up from her seat and pointing to the eighteenth green. "They're here, they're here!"

Convinced that his wife had become delusional, Will squinted down the fairway. His jaw dropped as he spied in the distance a crowd of spectators surrounding the green, waving and applauding as the contestants pulled up to the tee.

"What the . . . ?"

"They're our supporters, darling," Myrtle explained. "Here to cheer us on to victory!"

Will felt a sudden surge of manly pride. "They must have heard how I was tearing up the course, and came to see for themselves . . . ."

A sheepish grin crossed Myrtle's face. "Well . . . not exactly, Will. You see, before we teed off on ten, I called Gloria Fritz and asked her to arrange for some of the girls in the Women's Golf Association to show up when we came in. You know how you always fold on the back nine—how I always have to carry you on the last few holes? I assumed it would happen again, and that I could use all the help I could get at the finish! I never imagined you'd be playing so well and I'd be playing so poorly. But, as they say, no harm, no foul!"

Will looked up and realized that the cheering throng around the eighteenth green were all women. "But we don't need supporters," he groaned. "They don't belong here."

Unfortunately, there was nothing he could do. The Women's Golf Association had penetrated The Zone.

"What's the matter, Will?" Gus Goldman chortled after knocking his tee shot over the water into the center of the fairway. "Need *the ladies* to help you win?"

As Will stepped up to the tee, the sun disappeared behind a cloud, and a chill wind lashed his face. His knees buckled, his throat tightened and his hands began to shake. The hazard—a one hundred fifty yard carry — seemed to stretch from tee to green. All he could think of were the scores of skeptical female eyes trained upon him as he addressed the ball.

"They're everywhere," he murmured. "They're everywhere!"

●　　　●　　　●　　　●　　　●

The eighteenth hole of that year's Couples Better Ball Championship finals would become the stuff of legend at the Riverdale Golf and Country Club. The story of how Myrtle Anderson won the tournament by sinking a fifty-foot putt on the long par four, while her husband sat in their golf cart staring blankly into space like the victim of a high-speed collision, muttering inaudibly, would be told and retold for years to come — in the Ladies Locker Room, at the weekly lunches of the Women's Golf Association and wherever and whenever female members of the Club gathered.

For his part, Will claimed to have no recollection of that final hole. He could not remember, he said, knocking two balls into the water off the tee, hitting his approach into the front-side bunker, flailing helplessly at the buried lie in the sand or, lying eleven (or was it twelve?), finally picking up his ball and returning dejectedly to the cart. He also couldn't remember, he claimed, Myrtle's winning putt, or the cheering mob running onto the green, lifting her onto their shoulders and ecstatically carrying her off in triumph.

"But I do remember one thing," he told Ernie Evans as he sat in the safety of the Men's Locker Room Bar afterward nursing a double scotch. "I remember that, for awhile, I was in The Zone. You know how you hope and pray you can enter it just once in your life? How you yearn, just once, to be invincible? Well, let me tell you, Ernie, it's not all it's cracked up to be!"

"No, sir," he added, signaling the bartender to freshen his drink, "it's not all it's cracked up to be!"

THE COMPETITION

ACE

"Golf teaches that both success and failure are temporary. Golf also teaches that success is a lot more temporary."
Marc Gellman and Tom Hartman, in *Chicken Soup for the Golfer's Soul*

"Golf is a game that almost never fails, even at the highest levels on which it can be played, to mar a round with a lapse or two, and that at the other extreme rarely fails to grant even the most abject duffer, somewhere in his or her round, the wayward miracle of a good shot."
John Updike, *Golf Dreams*

When Howie Grossman stepped onto the ninth tee and absent-mindedly placed his ball between the gray stone markers, he wasn't thinking about his next shot. He wasn't worrying about the one hundred seventy-five yard carry to the pin, or the white stakes bordering the narrow fairway, or the yawning sand trap guarding the approach to the green. He was agonizing over whether he'd inadvertently parked his Toyota in a handicapped spot that morning.

So distracted was he, in fact, that he barely noticed the black-bordered sign posted beside the tee box:

RIVERDALE GOLF AND COUNTRY CLUB

Member/Guest Classic

HOLE-IN-ONE CONTEST

Fifty Thousand Dollars ($50,000) Awarded to First

Golfer to Shoot a HOLE-IN-ONE!

Brought to You Courtesy of River Grove Mortuary

"Your Final Stop on the Way Home" (R)

Even as he addressed his ball, executing his usual pre-swing routine—bending his knees, waggling his hips and flexing his deltoids—his mind wandered. He pondered what a nuisance his enormous gut had become, how it almost blocked his view of the ball and how some in River Grove still called him "Porky" in spite of his receding hairline and forty-odd years. Maybe they were right—maybe he should go on a diet, he mused as he brought his club back, swung down hard and, gouging out an immense divot, followed through, almost tumbling over.

Engulfed by the mid-morning sun, his ball disappeared from view. "Did anyone see that?" he called out.

"No, Howie," his partner replied. "But it sure sounded good."

As the foursome drove up to the green, Howie's thoughts turned to his ex-wife, Estelle. The struggling accountant wondered how he could come up with the $2,000 he needed for his next alimony payment. It was summer, slow as molasses, and cash wouldn't start flowing into his depleted coffers again until year-end. Maybe they could work something out.

Arriving at the green, Howie lumbered out of the cart and, shading his eyes against the glare of the sun, searched for his ball. It was nowhere in sight. The players spanned out, combing the sand traps, the ice plant, the bushes out-of-bounds. Finally, someone jokingly suggested they check the hole.

And there, nestled at the bottom of the cup like a long-forgotten Easter egg, lay a battered golf ball with the initials "HG" penned in red magic marker.

The ensuing green-side hoopla paled in comparison with the accolades later accorded Howie at the awards ceremony. Receiving a standing ovation from over one hundred fellow golfers, he giddily accepted a blown-up, facsimile check for $50,000 from the President of River Grove Mortuary.

"This'll sure come in handy," the lucky golfer gushed as cameras flashed to record the once-in-a-lifetime event.

In accepting the prize, he thought nothing of the word "VOID" written across the face of the check. He also failed to notice the grim-faced competitor seated in the front row, who, arms folded, refused to stand up and cheer.

•   •   •   •   •

The next day, when Howie arrived at the mortuary to collect his money, he was greeted by Denise Crier, the Director of Operations.

"Good to see you, Porky... I mean, Howard," his prematurely gray, former high school classmate chirped, leading him into her mahogany-encased office. "What can I do for you?   We're running a two-for-one special on pine caskets...."

"Sorry, Denise," he interrupted.   "I'm not here to bury anyone. I came to collect my fifty thousand dollars."

Met with a blank stare, Howie informed her of his accomplishment.

"Cudoos!" she bubbled.   "Who would have thought...?"

"May I have my check, please?" he asked politely.

It unfortunately fell upon Ms. Crier to inform her visitor that, while sponsoring the contest, the mortuary was not—technically speaking—answerable for the prize money. "That's the responsibility of Hole-in-One Incorporated—the contest insurer," she explained, rustling through a desk drawer.   "Now where did I put that address and phone number?"

Howie sighed. "But the sign said it was your contest."

"Ah—here it is!" she blurted out, extracting a rumpled scrap of paper and handing it to him.   "And the sign said 'brought to you courtesy of....'   Our lawyers were very particular about that!"

Howie grimaced as he read the South Florida address and toll-free telephone number scrawled on the paper. "I don't suppose they have an office nearby?" he asked forlornly.

That afternoon, after pressing a succession of ones, twos and pound-signs on his touch-tone phone, Howie finally reached Joel Haggarty, Vice President—Marketing of Sports Contests International, the parent company of Hole-in-One Incorporated.

"Well, congratulations, Mr. ... er ... Grossbaum," he chimed. "Now, all we need is your completed questionnaire, signed, witnessed and notarized, and, in no time, we'll mail your first check for ... uh ... let me see ... one thousand five hundred seventy-nine dollars and twenty cents ...."

"One thousand five hundred seventy-nine dollars and twenty cents?" Howie asked, wincing. "I thought I won fifty thousand!"

There was a pause. "Why, you did, Mr. Grossbaum. That's the first of the twenty annual installments to which you are entitled ... less, of course, applicable withholding taxes and our modest administrative fees."

Howie dropped the receiver onto the floor, then banged his head against the desktop as he fumbled to retrieve it.

"But the sign said ...."

"Sign, Mr. Grossbaum? What sign? Hole-in-One Incorporated didn't authorize any signs!"

"I don't suppose we could work something out?" Howie half-heartedly inquired.

After trying to discount the obligation at River Grove National Bank ("Are you kidding, Porky? Surely, you didn't expect us to take a Miami P.O. Box and a 1-800 number as collateral!"), Howie did as instructed. He filled out the five-page, single-spaced questionnaire (in triplicate), had it witnessed and sworn to, and mailed it back in the envelope provided.

Well, no harm, no foul, he thought, clutching the endorsed check as he stood in line to deposit it at the bank.

"Sorry, I'm closed," the young teller clucked, thrusting a "Next Window Please" sign in his face when he arrived at the counter.

•   •   •   •   •

Unassuming, protective of his privacy, Howie was nevertheless curious when Janet Needleman, self-described "human interest" reporter for *The River City Times*, called to request an interview.

"We're doing a piece about contest winners—you know, folks who've won the lottery, hit it big at Belmont, broken the bank in Monte Carlo. We want to know how their good fortune has affected their lives."

Deciding a little favorable publicity might be good for business, Howie agreed to meet the reporter for lunch. Sitting at a corner table awaiting her arrival, he rehearsed the answers to the questions he anticipated. "It was nothing. I'm just an ordinary bean-counter, not a golf pro." "The money and recognition haven't changed me. I'm still the same, hard-working guy I've always been." "Business is booming, but, of course, I could always use a little more."

Janet Needleman, it turned out, was, far from the stern, bespectacled harridan Howie had expected, a ravishing redhead with an engaging smile. Feeling light-headed after two glasses of White Zinfandel, he told the newspaperwoman to "fire away."

"Mr. Grossman," she began, punching the "ON" button of her tape recorder, "how do you respond to your ex-wife's charges that you're a deadbeat?"

Howie choked on his wine, spitting a mouthful onto the white linen tablecloth. "A what?" he gasped, his face beet-red.

"A deadbeat. Estelle claims you're in arrears on your alimony, that you haven't returned her phone calls for months, that . . . ."

"But what does that have to do with golf?"

"Golf?" the reporter blurted out, causing not a few heads to turn in their direction. "This isn't about golf, Mr. Grossman. It's about *you*."

The soon-to-be-famous weekend golfer spent the balance of the lunch explaining that business was often slow, that sometimes he'd find himself a little short, but that he'd never intentionally stiffed Estelle, and that, honestly, he'd always forked over the money eventually . . . .

"And, Mr. Grossman," the reporter pursued, "now that you're fifty thousand dollars richer, can you promise prompt payment in the future?"

Howie felt like a Titleist sculled once too often by its owner. "Well . . . uh . . . it's not that simple," he stammered, too embarrassed to reveal the truth about his winnings.

"I guess you're going to print all this?" he later asked, plunking down sixty dollars to cover the check. "I don't suppose we could work something out?"

Howie was not surprised, therefore, to read Janet Needleman's piece in the *Times*:

> When questioned about allegations of repeated failures to pay alimony [the article, entitled "Lucky Winner – or Born Loser?", revealed], the portly accountant fidgeted and squirmed. "It's not that simple," he claimed, without offering details.

"Howie, what's this about not paying your alimony?" his biggest client called to ask. "I can't have a welching accountant!"

Within a week, Howie was served a notice from Estelle's lawyer advising him that, unless he responded within ten days, his cash and accounts (including his Hole-in-One winnings) would be attached. The next day, the IRS informed him that his last three tax returns were being audited to verify his alimony deductions. His mailbox that day also housed appeals for funds from the Sierra Club, the Boy Scouts of America and WPUB, the local public television station, each mercifully addressed to "Occupant."

•   •   •   •   •

As it turned out, Howie was not the only golfer to score a hole-in-one that fateful day. Another high school classmate, Jack McHugh – the disgruntled player sitting in the front row at the awards ceremony – had replicated the feat a half hour later, going on, with his partner, to take the tournament crown. Unfortunately, McHugh – a PI lawyer, not one to suffer setbacks lightly – resented not only losing the hole-in-one contest, but having his thunder stolen in the process by "that lard-laden non-entity, Porky Grossman."

An attorney more concerned with victory than with truth, McHugh promptly launched an investigation into Howie's hole-in-one. He got Howie's playing partner to admit that, upon reflection, he couldn't say *for sure* that the auditor hadn't teed off in front of the markers, and that, the prior Christmas, he'd given his friend a set of "super-charged" titanium irons, not approved by the USGA, that *just might* have been in his bag that morning.

But it was Janet Needleman's *Times* article that broke the case for the lawyer. Applying standard deposition techniques, McHugh forced Bill Davidson, Riverdale's Treasurer, to reveal that Howie had not submitted his entry fee check until after the deadline. "I was just cutting the poor slob some slack," Howie's fellow divorcee confessed. "Misery loves company."

"You sniveling sandbagger!" McHugh barked as Howie waddled out of the locker room shower the following Saturday.

Certain this outburst was another manifestation of his success, Howie tried to act nonchalant. "Are you referring to me?"

"You bet I am, Porky! You should never have won that $50,000 prize. It rightfully belongs to me. You cheated!"

As McHugh rambled on, Howie's mind wandered back to his high school days when, scorned by McHugh and his football playing buddies, he'd offered to do their geometry homework for them in an effort to curry their favor. They'd gladly accepted his help. What good had that ever done for the failing accountant they still called "Porky?"

"Porky," McHugh barked, "I'm challenging you to a shootout?"

"A what?"

"A shootout. Closest to the pin on the ninth hole—winner takes all!"

Howie stood naked before his accuser, dripping wet, wrapped only in a fluffy white towel borrowed from the Club's linen closet. Conniving businessmen, a nosey reporter, a grasping ex-wife, a greedy tax collector, and now, a resentful rival mired in adolescence. Was there no end to those wanting a piece of him? Was there anything left to give?

"Sounds good," he replied to a startled McHugh. "Now, what about the stakes . . . ?"

• • • • •

Held the following Friday, and attended by a smattering of Riverdalers who'd learned of it through the clubhouse rumor mill, the shootout was straightforward: each player would be permitted five shots, the one closest to the pin the winner.

An air of excitement gripped the small gallery as the contestants pulled up to the tee and stepped out of the cart into the early morning mist. While the tall, slender McHugh, dressed in a crisp white golf shirt and freshly-pressed tan slacks, warmed up with a series of jumping jacks, windmills and squat thrusts, Howie, garbed in baggy Bermudas and a tattered sweat shirt with a faded "EVERLAST" printed across the front, leaned on his four iron and watched.

"Hey, what are you guys playing for?" someone shouted.

Howie straightened himself and addressed the spectators. "If Jack wins," he said, "he gets everything I won. If I win, he doubles it!"

With that, Ace Grossman turned to his opponent, raised his club to his shoulder, pointed it at him like an Uzi and squeezed an imaginary trigger. Teeing up, he took his stance, looked into the rising sun and swung mightily, all the while thinking how lucky he'd been to find the handicapped spot vacant that morning.

CHARITY

SECOND CHANCES

"I don't even know if there was a Mulligan. But he gave his name to a wonderful gesture."
Rex Lardner, *Out of the Bunker and into the Trees*

Everybody loved Joyce Jameson. Coordinator of Special Events at the Riverdale Golf and Country Club, Joyce was in charge of the myriad of outside functions held there each year, arranging everything from publicity and staffing to catering and prizes. A natural organizer, she had an uncanny ability to please.

But it was as "the Mulligan Lady" that the feisty widow endeared herself to the world. No charity golf outing was complete without the short, silver-haired Joyce, perched behind the registration desk alongside the first tee, decked out in a cotton blouse and Bermuda shorts, hawking her "mulligans"—the two-dollar tickets permitting golfers of all ages, sizes and levels of skill to replay errant shots without punishment or penalty. A true believer in charitable causes, she could convince even the most tight-fisted golfer that the purchase of a mulligan was critical to curing AIDS or to conquering poverty. "Besides, everyone's entitled to a second chance," she'd say, peeling her tickets off an enormous roll and depositing the player's money in a battered old cigar box.

But, never satisfied, the well-meaning Joyce was always seeking new ways to, in her words, "increase the Lord's take."

"Golfers will do anything to win," she told the Club's Board of Directors one winter afternoon, reporting on her money-raising activities during the prior year. "That's why we should broaden our product line."

"Product line?" exclaimed Ross Griswald, the portly Chairman. "We're a country club, not a conglomerate. We don't have a product line!"

"I mean," she explained, handing out a neatly-typed memorandum to the puzzled-looking Board members, "that we should increase the number of second chances we offer."

Joyce's proposal was simple. Rather than permitting golfers to buy just two "standard" mulligans — one for the front nine, one for the back nine — players would be allowed to purchase up to eight "multi-purpose" mulligans, usable on any hole not only to replay a wayward shot, but also to drop a ball out of a hazard, to treat a short putt as a "gimme," to hit from out-of-bounds or to use in place of a penalty stroke.

Everyone was impressed with the idea — everyone, that is, except Ernie Evans, the Club's veteran pro. "You're pretty confident for someone who's never played golf," he chided his old colleague.

Joyce shook her head in mock frustration. "Ah, the distinguished Doctor Evans weighs in," she said playfully. "Always the skeptic . . . ."

Evans cringed. The lanky, white-haired widower hated when Joyce called him "Doctor."

"I'm not a skeptic," he said defensively. "I just think your scheme may be flawed . . . ."

"Ernie," Joyce interrupted, "just stick to golf and leave charity to me."

"But that's what I'm worried about," he persisted. "People may give more, but they won't be playing golf. Bad lies and tricky putts are part of the game. You can't just let players buy their way out of trouble. It'll make things too easy."

"But that's the point," Joyce insisted. "We want everyone to have fun, not get stressed out. Besides, how could anyone be against something that not only helps charity, but is itself an act of charity — an expression of forgiveness and redemption. Ernie, you don't have to be a golfer to know this is a winner!"

Although unconvinced, Evans reluctantly withdrew his opposition. After all, he told himself, where charity was concerned, allowances had to be made.

•　　•　　•　　•　　•

The new mulligan was introduced at the annual Riverdale Roundup, a two-person team event sponsored by the local

Multiple Sclerosis Society. With Joyce dispensing tickets beneath a brightly-colored banner proclaiming "SUPPORT CHARITY AND WIN," sales were brisk. Not only did the "multi-purpose" mulligan raise over $1,000 (three times the normal take), the novelty proved immensely popular. It was soon adopted by other charities, who flocked to Riverdale to get in on the fund-raising action.

There were some complaints. A few (mostly busy executives) groused that the ready availability of second chances slowed play, or disrupted the "natural flow" of a match; others (mostly expert golfers) said that Joyce's creation, by permitting players to avoid difficult shots, took the joy out of the game. But these problems paled in comparison to the additional money suddenly pouring into charity coffers. "You see," Joyce boasted, waving a fistful of bills at Evans after one successful tournament, "I've always said golfers just want to win. Here's the proof!"

The pro scratched his head. "Joyce, you may know what golfers *want*, but you don't appreciate how they *think*. They're more complicated than you realize . . . ."

"Oh, Ernie, give me a break!" she scoffed. "This is charity at its best."

And, once again, the pro—hard-pressed to challenge Joyce's motives—did just that.

•　　•　　•　　•　　•

The first inkling of a problem came with the annual mid-summer golf outing of the Legal Aid Society. After pitching the virtues of the multi-purpose mulligan to a meeting of the organization, Joyce discovered that her brainchild had its detractors, particularly among those who considered themselves "sensitive" golfers.

"I don't see how we can support this," argued one young lawyer garbed in worn-out dungarees and a tee-shirt. "The system gives an unfair advantage to affluent players. Not everyone can afford to buy eight mulligans, you know!"

"Nonsense!" a graying attorney in a three-piece suit countered. "The system levels the playing field among golfers of differing abilities. It's not discriminatory . . . ."

After extended debate, the members narrowly approved Joyce's proposal. Receipts for the event, however, were significantly less than anticipated. "So what?" Joyce told Evans. "It's just a temporary setback. Anyway, what do lawyers know about charity?"

But others soon joined in the chorus of criticism. No matter what the event, someone would complain that the multi-purpose mulligan was "unfair" — that it unduly favored older golfers over younger golfers, high handicappers over low handicappers, short hitters over long hitters, bad putters over good putters. Joyce always prevailed by pleading with the dissidents to "consider the good of the charity." Nevertheless, attendance at events gradually shrank, and the money flowing into Joyce's cash box dwindled, as those who considered themselves disadvantaged (or sympathetic with those who were) stayed home.

The controversy came to a head with the "Beat Breast Cancer" tournament sponsored by the American Cancer Society. Traditionally pitting sixty-four men against sixty-four women, the mid-September contest, known as the "Battle of the Sexes," had always been an immensely popular community event.

The problem arose when Clint Wells, the former President of the local chapter, claimed that Joyce's system favored women over men. "I'm no male chauvinist," he asserted to the organization's Board, "but everybody knows that, generally speaking, men are better golfers than women. The . . . uh . . . er . . . ladies are more likely to hit bad tee shots, knock balls into hazards or miss short putts."

"Baloney," countered Edna Farber, the current President. "Differences in ability are already compensated for in handicaps. Besides, every player — regardless of sex — can purchase the same number of mulligans for the same price. There's perfect equality."

Wells (rumored to be bitter about losing the Presidency to his female rival) organized a "boycott of conscience," encouraging would-be golfers to contribute the $75 entry fee to the charity without participating in the event. "I'd rather do that than associate myself with something so blatantly discriminatory."

133

The boycott was effective. The tournament attracted only forty players—twenty men, twenty women—and receipts plummeted. To make matters worse, a dispute arose when a female player used a mulligan "gifted" to her by a teammate to drop out of a water hazard on the last hole. Joyce ruled that the gift was permitted, providing the margin of victory for the women. "Gifting is what this tournament is all about," she explained to the disgruntled captain of the men's team.

The following week, Joyce learned that the Society had voted to move its early October "Beat Prostate Cancer" event to the Riverdale Municipal course. The multi-purpose mulligan was history.

•　　•　　•　　•　　•

"I just don't understand," Joyce confessed to Ernie Evans at lunch shortly after the Cancer Society debacle. "I was only trying to help . . . ."

Evans idly picked at his cobb salad. "You shouldn't feel bad. I've spent over forty years trying to understand golfers, and I'm still not sure what makes them tick!"

Joyce smiled sadly. "Well, one thing's for sure," she said. "They don't leave their feelings in the clubhouse. They take them onto the golf course with them."

Evans was unable to suppress a chuckle. "They're only human, Joyce. And, like everyone else, they don't adapt well to change. Alter the rules on them and they're lost."

"Anyway," she sighed, "I won't have to worry about that anymore. I've resigned, you know."

Evans sat up straight and removed something from his shirt pocket. "I almost forgot," he said, handing it to Joyce. "The Board asked me to return this. It's your resignation. It wasn't accepted."

"But why not? I made a terrible mistake . . . ."

The pro shrugged, feigning ignorance. "I guess they're giving you a mulligan!" he said.

Joyce laughed, folding the letter neatly and placing it into her handbag.

"But," Evans added, "there is one condition."

"What?"

"That, from now on, you stick to charity and let me make the rules about golf tournaments."

Joyce nodded her head. "I understand," she replied with a faint smile. "In other words, Doctor, when it comes to golf — and golfers — I should leave it to the pros."

The victorious old pro gazed fondly at his incorrigible nemesis. "Uh, yeah . . . something like that," he muttered, swallowing hard.

It was hard not to feel charitable toward the Mulligan Lady.

THE REWARDS

THE LOOPER

"In Scotland he is as much of an institution as the player himself. He has grown up on the links, and is the guide, counselor, and friend of the player whose clubs he carries. One of his principal qualifications there is that he should be able to conceal his contempt for your game."
H.E. Howland, in Golf Talk

"The kid shook his head and said, 'Golf is nothing but a microcosm of life.'
'It ain't no microcosm of nothin',' protested the Goose. 'It's a damn game.'"
Bo Links, *Riverbank Tweed and Roadmap Jenkins: Tales from the Caddie Yard*

"Don't you think it's about time we sold that old thing," complained Betty Donovan, turning out the light and slipping into bed. "It's not doing anyone any good just sitting there, gathering dust."

"Must you bring that up again?" groaned her husband, Tom, lying on his back, staring at the ceiling. "I don't care how much it's worth. I just can't see letting go of it . . . It's almost a part of me."

"Like that thick skull of yours!" she replied, turning away and yanking the covers over her head.

Once again, the Donovan's were arguing over the trophy in their living room—the 1947 Waterfield Cup, won by Sammy Sanders and given to Tom, his caddy in that year's American Golf Classic. Like an unwelcome relation, the silver-plated bowl—believed by many of their friends to be potentially worth thousands in the sports memorabilia market—was a source of constant bickering between the childless couple.

"Sammy said I deserved the Cup more than he did," the retired groundskeeper would explain to curious visitors. "If I hadn't talked him into using a five iron, rather than a six, on the last hole, he'd never have won the tournament. He told everyone that I was the real champion."

"Champion my foot," the short, plump Betty would chide after their guests had left. "That trophy's just a reminder that you never amounted to anything. Just think about it—the most important thing you ever did was carry another man's golf clubs around. A looper, for God's sake! You should be ashamed of yourself."

After a while, the slight, white-haired Tom would just shrug and walk away. But that evening, lying next to Betty, he tossed and turned for hours.

•　　•　　•　　•　　•

The next morning, to appease his wife, Tom took the Cup to River City to be appraised.

"Normally," the appraiser told him, "a piece like this would go for five—maybe six-thousand. But this is unique. Since the American Golf Classic was discontinued in 1948, it's one of a kind. And it's in reasonable condition—a little tarnished, maybe, but no major cuts, scratches or dents."

A frown crossed Tom's craggy face. "What's it worth?" he asked, not really wanting to know.

"Conservatively, I'd say fifteen thousand—maybe twenty," the appraiser replied. "If it's genuine, that is," he quickly added.

Driving home, Tom couldn't get his mind off the trophy. He remembered that afternoon in 1947 when, as a fourteen-year-old caddie, he'd helped Sammy Sanders hoist the Cup while news photographers snapped pictures and excited spectators cheered. "Someday, Tom, you'll win this," the legendary pro had told him. He also remembered the day, five years later, when a package arrived at the base hospital enclosing the trophy and Sammy's letter, addressed to "The Pluckiest Looper I've Ever Known," telling him "it's all yours." That was after Tom lost an eye in a skirmish near the Thirty-Eighth Parallel.

Maybe Betty was right. He did have a blind spot where that trophy was concerned. And he'd certainly never amounted to much in life. Although Course Superintendent at the

Riverdale Golf and Country Club for almost thirty years, he was just a glorified gardener, working under professional agronomists, landscape architects and environmental engineers. Maybe it was time he did something for himself and for Betty. Selling the Cup would more than pay for the trip to Europe he'd been promising her for years.

•   •   •   •   •

Betty was delighted with the appraiser's report, as well as with Tom's reluctant decision to auction off the trophy. Hoping to stimulate interest, she arranged for an article about the Cup to appear in *The River City Times*.

> *As a boy [the piece began], helping his family make ends meet by working weekends as a caddie, Tom Donovan dreamed of becoming a professional golfer, of joining the ranks of Bobby Jones, Gene Sarazen and Walter Hagen in the pantheon of Golf's Immortals. At sixteen, he won the State Junior Golf title; at seventeen, he reached the semi-finals of the National Amateur. But Tom's dream was shattered one September morning in Korea when an errant American mortar shell struck his position. Partially blinded, he was never able to play again. But, according to his friend and mentor, golfing great Sammy Sanders, the young war hero was already a champion.*

The story was quickly picked up by other papers and eventually carried by all the major news services and broadcast networks.

•   •   •   •   •

On the morning before the auction, while Tom was admiring the trophy one last time, the doorbell rang. He walked over to the bay window, pulled back the lace curtains and peered outside. There he saw, standing at the door, a tall, middle-aged woman clutching a bulky plastic shopping bag. Although his vision often played tricks on him, he was certain he had seen her face before.

"Good morning, Mr. Donovan," she said hesitantly when he opened the door. "My name is Anne McCarthy. May I have a word with you?"

Tom led her into the living room. "What can I do for you?"

The woman shifted about uneasily in her chair. "Mr. Donovan," she said, "I'm not sure how to begin. You see, I came here from River City after reading about the Waterfield Cup in the papers."

"Are you interested in buying it?" Tom said with a boyish grin. "It's a bit pricey — and I'm only taking cash!"

"Oh, no," she replied, flustered. "It's not that ... it's just ...." She reached into her bag and removed a silver-plated trophy seemingly identical to that on the mantelpiece.

"Perhaps you'd better explain," Tom said as he sat down to examine it.

"Well, you see, I'm Anne *Sanders* McCarthy. Sammy Sanders was my father ...."

Tom's mind raced back to the American Golf Classic of 1947, and to the scrawny young girl Sammy had introduced to his caddy as his daughter. "I thought I recognized you," he finally said. "Your father was a wonderful man."

She nodded. "Yes, and generous to a fault. It was just like him to give you the Waterfield Cup. The only problem," she added, pointing to the trophy she'd brought, "is that you're holding the real Waterfield Cup in your hands."

Tom looked up, startled. "That can't be right."

"I'm afraid it is," she sighed. "Just look at the inscription on the side."

Tom strained to read the words. "But something's wrong ...."

"Now compare this," she continued, removing a crumpled-up photograph from the bag. It was an enlargement of the news photo of Tom standing next to Sammy Sanders, holding the Waterfield Cup in the air, the inscription clearly visible.

AMERICAN GOLF CLASSIC

1947 Champion

Samuel N. Saunders

"You see, when Dad heard you'd been wounded, he decided to give you the Cup as a token of his appreciation. He'd always said you were the one who really won that tournament. But when he took it off the shelf, he noticed the misspelling. I guess because Dad had won on the very last hole, the engraver was a little hasty in completing his work. Anyway, the inscription couldn't be changed without permanently damaging the Cup, and since the tournament was no longer being held, Dad couldn't get an official replacement. Well, you know what a perfectionist he was; he said you were the same way. He had another trophy made—one that wasn't flawed—one he said you could be proud of. That's the one he gave you."

Tom leaned back, shaking his head. "In other words, my trophy is worthless!"

"Oh, no, not worthless," she protested. "I mean, only in monetary terms . . . ."

"I see . . . ."

"Well, when Dad passed away, the Cup became the property of the charitable foundation he'd established to promote youth golf. After the news reports came out, the Trustees discussed the situation and decided that the original trophy was rightfully yours. So they've authorized me to exchange it for the one Dad gave you. Believe it or not, the misspelling actually makes it more valuable. It's like a misprinted stamp or dollar bill."

Tom stood up, shaking his head. He handed the trophy back to his visitor. "Thank you, Mrs. McCarthy, but I really don't want this."

"But why not?'

Tom smiled. "You see, I always believed that I owned the real trophy—the one that your father said really belonged to me. And nothing you've said has changed my mind. I think you should just return that one to the foundation. I'm sure it has better uses for it than I do."

"You don't believe me?"

"Of course I believe you."

"Then you know you can't sell the trophy Dad gave you."

"I guess, deep down, I've always known that," he replied, taking his own trophy off the mantelpiece. "The money would have been nice. And, trust me, my wife isn't going to be pleased. But I'd rather keep this one. You see, I've become very attached to it. Flawed or not, it's mine."

"By the way," he added as they said good-bye at the door, "I'd appreciate it if you never told anyone about the foundation's offer — particularly Mrs. Donovan!"

•   •   •   •   •

Today, the Waterfield Cup won by Tom Donovan remains on display in his living room. He proudly cleans and polishes it every day, more the perfectionist than ever. To his surprise, Betty — apparently impressed with his acceptance of what she calls "a bad break" — has ceased her nagging.

"There's another version of this thing kicking around," he now tells visitors. "Some wealthy collector up in River City bought it for fifty thousand dollars. Money's helped a lot of kids."

"But this is the genuine article," the aging looper adds, a twinkle in his good eye. "Yessir, the real thing."

THE FELLOWSHIP

OUTSIDE THE BOX

"I don't want to belong to any club that would have me as a member."

Groucho Marx

"Isn't it terrific?" crowed Ross Griswald, leaning precariously over the glass countertop, peering at the computer screen in the back of the pro shop. "Our own website: CountryClub.com. Now, with just the touch of a key, or the click of a mouse, anyone can find out who we are and what we're all about!"

"The Board is to be congratulated for its cutting-edge thinking," chirped Joyce Jameson, the silver-haired Coordinator of Special Events, donning her glasses to get a better view. "And how fortunate the name wasn't taken . . . ."

"Maybe nobody else had the guts to use it," countered Ernie Evans, seated at the keyboard, shaking his head as he scanned the glitzy Home Page. "Seems a bit pompous to me—like we're the one and only country club around!"

"Actually, Ernie," boasted Dennis Chaudaire, at that moment striding into the pro shop, a self-satisfied grin on his face, "we bought the name for a song from a club outside Chicago that went belly-up last year."

The pro turned to the boyish-looking General Manager, his brow furrowed. "That's comforting."

Evans clicked on the mouse and brought up a page entitled "MISSION STATEMENT."

"Hmm—interesting," he said, pointing the cursor at the third paragraph. "Did you write this, Dennis?"

> *The Riverdale Golf and Country Club is a private club with a public mission. Known for its unwavering support of civic and charitable causes, its leadership in promoting conservation and the protection of the environment, and its unflinching commitment to diversity, Riverdale is a treasured*

community asset. As we move into the Twenty-First Century, the Club remains dedicated to the values of good citizenship, neighborliness and inclusiveness that have characterized its long and distinguished history.

The young General Manager reddened noticeably as all eyes turned in his direction. "What's wrong with that?" he asked.

"Civic involvement, environmental protection, diversity . . . ?"

"The buzzwords of the New Millennium," Chaudaire replied. "Absolutely essential if we're to attract the younger generation (and its disposable income) to our Club. And a completely appropriate way to kick off our new public relations campaign!"

The lanky, white-haired pro arched his eyebrows. "Dennis, I've been around a tad longer than you, and I wouldn't swear to the veracity of that write-up. Plus, it has nothing to do with golf, tennis or swimming. Besides, as this thing says, we're a *private* club . . . ."

The Chairman rapped his chubby knuckles on the counter. "Cut it out, you two. Bickering among the staff isn't going to help our fall membership drive."

Griswald turned to Evans. "Ernie, sometimes we old timers get a little too set in our ways. Doing something 'outside the box' might be good for a change. Why don't we give Dennis's idea a chance?"

The pro shrugged. "Well, I've always said people shouldn't go where they don't belong. And public relations isn't in my job description . . . ."

"You're right there!" Chaudaire interrupted.

"So," the pro sighed, "I'll just keep quiet — and wish you all luck in cyberspace."

With that, Evans turned away and gazed out the window at the overcast October sky. Here we go again, he thought as he watched autumn's first leaves blow by in the wind.

•　　　•　　　•　　　•　　　•

True to his word, Ernie Evans stayed out of the Club's public relations campaign. He made no comment when Riverdale was soon inundated with applications for new charity events, including a gala dinner hosted by Gimme Shelter, a local foundation for the homeless (to be attended by over one hundred of its "clients") and a golf tournament sponsored by the Halfway House Association (for which many of its temporarily incarcerated "residents" would serve as volunteers). He also kept mum when, employing the site's electronic bulletin board as a forum, the River Grove chapter of Save Our Planet lobbied the Club to use recycled waste water for irrigation "in a manner consistent with your purported 'leadership' in conservation" and the Municipal League petitioned the Club to oppose a new office complex proposed by developer and long-time member Wendell McGill, citing "Riverdale's professed interest in the environment."

But the membership application of Jerome A. Stein proved an entirely different matter.

Arriving in late October, the application seemed, at first, to be perfectly routine. The typewritten form identified the applicant as a "media personality" in his mid-forties, living with his wife and three children in the ritzy Forest Park section of River Grove. Seeking full "family" membership privileges at Riverdale, it included the required information concerning education (two years at River City University), income (over $1 million per year), outside interests and activities (pick-up basketball and croquette) and other club memberships (stated as "Not Applicable"). A black-and-white photograph disclosed the applicant to be a slightly-built, mousy-looking, balding man with thick glasses and a pencil moustache.

Suspicions were aroused, however, by the applicant's unusual list of "references." These included a lady by the name of "Good Time Sal," a trio identified as "Dan the Dwarf," "Mike the Moron" and "the King of the Hood," and someone (or something) of unknown gender referred to as "Liberace's Revenge."

A quick investigation revealed the pedestrian-looking applicant to be none other than infamous radio shock jock, Jerry Stein, self-styled "Ruler of the Airwaves," host of "The Morning Menagerie" on WRIV-FM, the "Talk Station of the People."

"I'll be damned if I'll let Jerry Stein join Riverdale," thundered Ross Griswald as Evans, abruptly summoned to an "emergency" staff meeting, strode into the Chairman's office. Seated before Griswald, resembling bereaved relations at a wake, were Joyce Jameson, Dennis Chaudaire and Tom Trailer, the Chairman's son-in-law and the Club's sometime legal counsel.

"I've got nothing against free speech," Griswald insisted. "As far as I'm concerned, that garbage-mouthed deejay can say anything he wants to on the air. But that doesn't mean I have to associate with him and those freaks and nut cases he hangs out with. We've got standards, you know!"

Nods of approval greeted this assertion, "inclusiveness" apparently having its limits.

"Now, Tom," the Chairman continued, turning to the gaunt-looking attorney, "I assume we're on solid legal ground here."

"Uh . . . er . . . yes . . . at least I think so, Dad—I mean, sir," stammered Trailer, squirming like a first-year law student queried by an overbearing contracts professor.

The Chairman glared at the lawyer. "What do you mean, you think so?"

Grimacing, Trailer reached into his briefcase and extracted a sheaf of papers.

"This is a letter we received yesterday from Mr. Stein," he announced glumly, passing out copies to those assembled. "It says he's applying for membership not only for himself and his wife and children, but 'on behalf of those who comprise my extended radio family, many of whom I expect to invite to your Club as my guests on a regular basis.'"

Griswald grunted in disgust while the others sat in stunned silence.

The lawyer cleared his throat. "He goes on to say that his application 'will test your alleged commitment to diversity,' and that, 'if you reject me, you will be rejecting my entire on-air family, demonstrating that your so-called 'Mission Statement' is a sham!'"

The portly Chairman angrily crumpled the letter into a ball and hurled it into the wastebasket. "Balderdash," he huffed. "Isn't the law on our side?"

Trailer fidgeted with his collar and tie. "Well, the cases clearly hold that state anti-discrimination laws don't apply to private organizations. On the other hand, the courts have also consistently applied those laws to 'civic' organizations. And calling yourself a 'community treasure' on your website isn't particularly helpful."

The scowling Chairman pounded his fist on the table, upsetting a can of diet soda, causing the petite Coordinator of Special Events to scamper out of her seat to avoid a drenching.

"He's not going to get away with it!" Griswald bellowed. "We'll take this all the way to the Supreme Court . . . !"

The pro reluctantly entered the fray. "Take it easy, Ross. The last thing we need is a lot of negative publicity. I'd rather have an infestation of snakes on the front nine than a pack of reporters investigating our membership practices."

"I'm not sure we can avoid it, Ernie," Trailer ventured sheepishly, reaching once more into his briefcase. "Phone messages from local reporters," he explained, displaying a handful of pink slips. "Seems Mr. Stein just announced his plans to join the Club on 'The Morning Menagerie.'"

Evans leafed through the messages and groaned. "Now we've done it," he said. "We're in the spotlight!"

•　　　•　　　•　　　•　　　•

"LOCAL SHOCK JOCK APPLIES FOR MEMBERSHIP IN UPSCALE SUBURBAN CLUB" read the headline of the *River City Times* "Entertainment" section the next morning. Evans, sitting alone in the snack bar having an English muffin and coffee, the paper spread before him, grimaced as he read the article, which was accompanied by a photo of Jerry Stein, decked out in a platinum blonde wig and gold-sequined gown, autographing copies of his take-no-prisoners autobiography (entitled *My World and Welcome to It*) at a local book signing.

> *Radio personality Jerry Stein – long known for his uninhibited conversational style and outrageous on-air antics – announced yesterday that he would be taking his "Crusade for the Great Unwashed" from the confines of his downtown broadcast studio into "the haven of the social and*

economic elite" by applying for membership in the exclusive Riverdale Golf and Country Club.

"I speak for the little guy," explained the confrontational deejay — famed for his lively early morning banter with a regular ensemble of self-described "strippers, lesbos, drunks, bangers, retards, louts, gimps and geeks" known as "Jerry's Kids" — "those the rich and powerful don't consider 'good enough' to have over for dinner, to live in their fashionable neighborhoods, to attend their fancy private schools or to join their exclusive clubs. My campaign to join Riverdale — a club cynically advertising its devotion to 'diversity' and 'inclusiveness' — will send a message to all snooty bleeding hearts that ordinary people are sick and tired of being jerked around!"

Many of the shock jock's loyal listeners agreed. "Stick it to 'em, Jerry," enthused regular caller "River City Roy." "It's time these country club do-gooders put up or shut up. We're behind you a hundred and ten percent!"

"Jerry Rules!" and "[Bleep] Riverdale" were sentiments expressed by many callers.

While agreeing that a successful lawsuit against the Club would be a long-shot, some experts note that Riverdale has not helped its legal position by making certain self-serving statements on its Internet website (which Stein credits for giving him the idea of applying for membership).

The Club declined comment.

As Evans shook his head in disbelief, Club member Mike Dagostino approached his table. "Is it true, Ernie?" he asked, pointing to the article. "Is Jerry Stein trying to join Riverdale?"

Evans calmly sipped his coffee. "Mike, you know I don't handle membership matters. You'll have to ask Joyce or Dennis about that."

Dagostino waved off the pro. "Oh, sure — like you don't know everything that goes on around here. Anyway, tell the Board the members will back them up one hundred and ten percent in telling this bozo to stick it."

"I'll give them the message," the pro replied, feeling a sudden chill in the air.

Evans returned to the pro shop, churning inside. Visions of outraged letters, boisterous pickets, daily media briefings and endless talk show blather swirled in his head as he tried to get back to work. Spotting his computer in the corner, the Club home page flickering on the screen, the pro gave it an angry kick. It crashed into blackness. Suddenly, he had an idea.

Booting up, the pro began searching the Internet for information about Jerry Stein. He soon uncovered scores of Web articles about the talk show host, most dealing with the media campaigns Stein had launched over the years in the name of his "Great Unwashed": "SHOCK JOCK ANNOUNCES CANDIDACY FOR GOVERNOR ON 'PEOPLE'S PARTY' TICKET—VOWS TO RESTORE DEATH PENALTY, LEGALIZE DRUGS AND REPAIR POTHOLES"; "RADIO PERSONALITY CALLS FOR ELIMINATION OF BANS ON PORNOGRAPHY, PUBLIC NUDITY AND SPITTING ON SIDEWALK"; "TALK SHOW HOST STEIN LEADS ARMY OF JOBLESS MIDGETS IN DISRUPTING TV AWARDS CEREMONY, DEMANDING FAIR TREATMENT FOR 'LITTLE GUY' IN ENTERTAINMENT INDUSTRY."

Perusing the articles, the pro soon made an interesting discovery. All of Stein's "crusades" seemed to follow a pattern: after attracting expressions of shock, horror and dismay from their targets, followed by a raucous media blitz—and a jump in Arbitron ratings—his forays against the "establishment" inevitably disappeared like a towering tee shot launched into a fog. One campaign replaced another, then was soon forgotten. Everything seemed almost scripted.

Evans called Ross Griswald. "I've got an idea, Ross. Let me take this guy on a tour of the Club. Maybe I can talk some sense into him before he takes this thing too far."

"What's your plan?"

"I'd rather not say. And, frankly, you'd rather not know. Let's just say it's the product of 'outside the box' thinking."

There was a prolonged pause. "And another thing, Ross," Evans added. "You'll have to make me temporary Membership Director.

Another pause ensued. "Um ... okay, Ernie," Griswald finally replied. "I'll trust you on this one."

After hanging up, Evans quickly made his way to the clubhouse supply closet to begin hatching his scheme.

• • • • •

The following afternoon, Ernie Evans paced nervously in the pro shop, awaiting his guest's arrival. On the countertop lay a stack of e-mails and faxes from irate Club members opposed to Jerry Stein's membership application, some employing language usually reserved for wayward drives and errant approach shots.

Evans had been surprised when Stein's producer readily agreed to the tour. "Might pick up some good material for the show," he had said, promising the shock jock's appearance promptly at three. "You know, some funny bits."

The pro was even more surprised when the vaunted "Ruler of the Airwaves" arrived by himself, sans entourage. Dressed in a conservative blazer and tie, eyes hidden beneath thick glasses, carrying an attache case in one hand and a cell phone in the other, Jerry Stein looked anything but the flamboyant talk show host he played on the air. Evans couldn't tell whether he was meeting the real Jerry Stein, or Jerry Stein in disguise.

"I hope this won't take long," Stein grumbled, glancing at his watch. "I've got to get back to the studio to do some commercial spots."

"Where's your troupe, Mr. Stein?" Evans asked. "Your side-kicks?"

Stein snickered. "Oh—you mean my props? I only use them when I'm performing. What you see is what you get!"

After loading the deejay into the Club's Hospitality Wagon, Evans took him on a guided tour of the golf course. As they rode along the bumpy cart paths, Evans proudly pointed out the expansive, ryegrass fairways, the lush, treacherous rough, the impeccably-manicured, undulating greens and the magnificent back nine vistas. Stein, taking the opportunity to review scripts and occasionally bark orders to subordinates on his cell phone, seemed unimpressed. "Uh . . . nice," he muttered distractedly between calls. "What's next?"

Pulling up to the fourteenth tee, Evans showed his visitor the stand of elms defining the hole's sharp dogleg right. "See those trees?" he said. "Most everyone plays around them. But there are some members who always try to hit over them! They usually don't succeed."

Stein momentarily looked up from his reading material. "Maybe they just want to test boundaries," he said matter-of-factly, "and enjoy the challenge."

At the eighteenth tee, the pro pointed to the scenic water hazard guarding the approach to the fairway.

"Makes you want to grab your clubs and start swinging, doesn't it?"

Stein, checking his watch again, shrugged indifferently. "Actually, I don't play golf. Never had the time."

Evans next took his guest to the tennis courts. "We just had them resurfaced," he said. "If you want, I can borrow some balls and racquets, and we can check them out!"

"As I said, I'm in kind of a hurry. Maybe some other time."

Similar reactions greeted the Club's Olympic-size swimming pool, its fully-equipped exercise room and its conference and dining facilities. Jerry Stein, when not preoccupied with other matters, simply listened in silence while the pro described the privileges available to Club members. Evans was thankful that at least there were no jibes, jokes, outbursts or put-downs.

"This is all real nice," Stein finally said as the pro led up the stairs to the clubhouse's second floor. "But it's about as exciting as a tour of a nursing home. Don't you have anything I can use on my show?"

Evans just smiled and opened a large oak door at the head of the stairs. "This is the Members Memorial Room," he announced as he led his guest into a dark, musty, wood-paneled room filled with old photographs, books on golf, plaques, trophies, antique clubs and other memorabilia.

"Kind of like a museum," Stein observed, picking up a rusting mashie-niblick from a rack on the wall and eyeing it like an ancient relic. "Or should I say mausoleum?" he corrected himself, blowing the dust off a tattered copy of the 1929 *Encyclopedia of Golf.*

"Call it what you will," replied the pro. "But I like to come up here to collect my thoughts."

Stein replaced the club in the rack, then turned to Evans. "Surely, Mr. Evans, you don't give a rat's ass what I think about your country club. Why did you invite me here today?"

Evans scratched his head. "Funny, I was going to ask you why you bothered to come."

"That's obvious," snapped the deejay. "You know what I want!"

The pro removed a golf ball from his pocket and began tossing it in the air, trying to appear nonchalant. "I'm not sure I do. You don't play golf or tennis, have no interest in the other facilities of the Club and seem to spend all your time working—or should I say, performing? You're all business. You don't actually want to join Riverdale, do you?"

Stein smiled stiffly. "Let's just say I'm like those guys who want to hit over the trees. I appreciate the challenge."

Evans laughed, then suddenly turned serious. "Well, I've always said you should be careful what you ask for: you might get it!"

With that, the pro led his visitor to a display panel on the opposite side of the room.

"What the hell is this?" Stein asked testily.

"It's our 'Members Roster'—a listing of all Riverdalers, past and present."

"Looks more like a mass gravestone to me. Got any bodies buried back there? Maybe members who got out of line?"

"Deceased members are indicated by asterisk," Evans replied, pointing to the names stenciled near the bottom of the list.

WILLIAM O. and DOROTHY SAGAN

THEODORE and MARSHA* SEABURY

TODD B. and ANNE SLATER*

JEROME A. and RACHEL STEIN

Stein gazed at the roster, then at the pro, his mouth agape. "You mean you guys are actually going to let me join this place?" he blurted out. "Just like that—without a fight?"

The pro returned the ball to his pocket. "If it were up to me, I'd fight you tooth and nail. An all-out war with the infamous Jerry Stein would liven this place up a bit. But we're pretty stodgy around here. Don't like our routine disrupted."

For the first time, Stein was visibly agitated. "But just throwing in the towel—I mean, what the hell good would that do me? There's no material in that—no ratings points! And I'd look like a damn fool!"

The pro smiled slyly. "Some might even say you were a hypocrite for joining," he chuckled. "But you, Mr. Stein, of all people, should know that publicity is a double-edged sword."

The deejay grimaced. "But I don't belong... *there*," he croaked, pointing to the Members Roster as if it were a most-wanted poster.

"What you see is what you get," said the pro.

The visitor's face turned red. "You know, I don't believe you for a minute. I think you're trying to trick me! This is all a lot of bull ...."

The pro raised his hand. "Maybe so, Mr. Stein, but can you afford to take that risk?"

Stein shook his head, then seemed to suppress a shiver. "Maybe we should talk ...." he said, checking his watch again.

•　　•　　•　　•　　•

The next morning, Jerry Stein's producer called Evans offering a deal to withdraw the shock jock's membership application. Stein cryptically announced his decision by explaining he had "other priorities." (Shortly thereafter, he began a new on-air campaign: to force the Cub Scouts to admit Good Time Sal as a Den Mother.) He never mentioned the Riverdale Golf and Country Club again. Neither his listeners nor the press seemed to notice.

The Riverdale Board—particularly its Chairman—were relieved. "I don't know how you did it, Ernie," Ross Griswald said afterward as the two stood in the pro shop watching a cold autumn rain soak the course.

"I guess some people just can't stand success," replied Evans. "Of course, we did have to agree to host the first annual Jerry Stein Celebrity Golf Outing next spring."

"God only knows who'll be competing in that."

"And to take down that self-congratulatory website. Good riddance, if you ask me!"

The Chairman began rocking back and forth on his heels, his eyes downcast, like a child caught misbehaving.

"We did take it down, didn't we, Ross?"

"Uh . . . er . . . not exactly. Actually, I had Dennis do a bit of rewriting . . . ."

"Oh, no," the pro exclaimed, rushing over to the computer and typing in "CountryClub.com." A single page emerged on the screen.

THE RIVERDALE GOLF AND COUNTRY CLUB

A private club serving the social and recreational needs of its members from River Grove and environs. For further information, call Ernie Evans at 812-555-1356.

"Well, it's not cutting edge, but at least it's the truth," said the Chairman as the pro shook his head and groaned.

THE END

Educators Discount Policy

To encourage use of our books for education, educators can purchase three or more books (mixed titles) on our standard discount schedule for resellers. See **sciencehumanitiespress.com/educator/educator.html** for more detail or call

Science & Humanities Press,

PO Box 7151, Chesterfield MO 63006-7151

636-394-4950

Our books are guaranteed:

If a book has a defect, or doesn't hold up under normal use, or if you are unhappy in any way with one of our books, we are interested to know about it and will replace it and credit reasonable return shipping costs. Products with publisher defects (i.e., books with missing pages, etc.) may be returned at any time without authorization. However, we request that you describe the problem, to help us to continuously improve.

Books by Charles Rechlin

Riverdale Chronicles--Charles F. Rechlin (2003). Life, living and character studies in the setting of the Riverdale Golf Club by Charles F. Rechlin 5½ X 8½, 160 pp ISBN: 1-888725-84-2 $14.95

Winners and Losers--Charles F. Rechlin (2005). a collection of humorous short stories portraying misadventures of attorneys, stock brokers, and others in the Urban workplace. 5½ X 8½, 198 pp. ISBN 1-59630-002-7 $14.95

Order form			
Item	Each	Quantity	Amount
Missouri (only) sales tax 6.925%			
Priority Shipping			$5.00
	Total		
Ship to Name:			
Address:			
City State Zip:			

BeachHouse Books
PO Box 7151
 Chesterfield, MO 63006-7151
(636) 394-4950
www.beachhousebooks.com

www.beachhousebooks.com

160